FOLLOW ME ON INSTAGRAM
@DYLANWRITESHORROR

DYLAN COLÓN

THIS HOUSE IS BROKEN

A RELIGIOUS HORROR NOVEL

EDITED BY VALORIE DALTON
BOOK COVER BY TRAVIS COOK

This House Is Broken
A Religious Horror Novel
By Dylan Colón

THIS NOVEL IS DEDICATED TO MY FAMILY, FRIENDS, CO-WORKERS, AND ANYBODY ELSE THAT BELIEVED IN ME. IT'S DEDICATED TO THOSE I LOST ALONG THE WAY. DAD, GRANDMA, POP POP, G-DADDY, GRANDPA, AND ALL THOSE I WILL FOREVER MISS... I'LL CONTINUE TO MAKE YOU PROUD!

THIS NOVEL IS FOR REGINA MCKIERNAN. I WAS THE ONLY CHILD HELD BACK FROM THE FIRST GRADE FOR BEING THE ONLY ONE WHO COULDN'T READ OR WRITE. YOU OPENED MY IMAGINATION THROUGH FANTASY AND TAUGHT ME HOW TO READ AND EXPRESS MYSELF!

MAMMA! DAD(FRANCIS)! TYLER! YOU NEVER GAVE UP ON ME EITHER! KAYRI MCCARTIN, YOU ARE ONE IN FEW OTHER TEACHERS TO ALWAYS SEE THE GREATNESS IN ME THAT I AM JUST NOW SEEING IN MYSELF THESE PAST FEW YEARS. I THANK ANYBODY AND EVERYBODY WHO PUSHED ME TO BE EXCELLENT. MY BROTHER, MICHAEL COLÓN BEING ANOTHER ONE!

THIS HOUSE IS BROKEN
A RELIGIOUS HORROR NOVEL
BY DYLAN COLÓN
COPYRIGHT © 2020 BY DYLAN COLÓN

ALL RIGHTS RESERVED. NO PART OF THIS PUBLICATION MAY BE REPRODUCED, DISTRIBUTED, OR TRANSMITTED IN ANY FORM OR BY ANY MEANS, OR STORED IN A DATABASE OR RETRIEVAL SYSTEM, WITHOUT PRIOR WRITTEN PERMISSION OF THE AUTHOR.

THE SCANNING, UPLOADING, AND DISTRIBUTION OF THIS BOOK VIA THE INTERNET OR VIA OTHER MEANS WITHOUT THE PERMISSION OF THE PUBLISHER IS ILLEGAL AND PUNISHABLE BY LAW. PLEASE PURCHASE ONLY AUTHORIZED ELECTRONIC EDITIONS AND DO NOT PARTICIPATE IN OR ENCOURAGE ELECTRONIC PIRACY OF COPYRIGHTED MATERIALS. YOUR SUPPORT OF THE AUTHOR'S RIGHTS IS APPRECIATED.

THIS IS A WORK OF FICTION. NAMES, CHARACTERS, PLACES, AND INCIDENTS ARE EITHER THE PRODUCT OF THE AUTHOR'S IMAGINATION OR USED FICTITIOUSLY. ANY RESEMBLANCE TO ACTUAL PERSONS, LIVING OR DEAD, EVENTS, OR LOCALES IS ENTIRELY COINCIDENTAL.

Broken Chapters

Chapter 1: Family Breakfast

Chapter 2: Happy Birthday

Chapter 3: Something Terrible

Chapter 4: Innocence

Chapter 5: Evelyn

Chapter 6: 4AM

Chapter 7: The Encounter

Chapter 8: The Reflection Room

Chapter 9: Days Later

Chapter 10: Grieving

Chapter 11: Thief

Chapter 12: Secret Thoughts

Chapter 13: Samuel

Chapter 1
Family Breakfast

The basement was pitch black, and Faith was terrified of it. Besides the fact that the basement door was locked, it was full of wooden tables upon which various tools were spread, immersed in spider webs, untouched since the day her father left. A tiny glass window half-buried in the ground provided the only light to the basement. At night, a dim street light made what was visible in the basement appear as something out of a horror movie, full of shadows.

Silence…

She couldn't hear a thing in this room. Her head was full of thoughts that would terrify a 12-year-old girl whose imagination was bolstered by any movie even slightly horrific, any book even slightly creepy. In the pitch black, the furniture in the room made dark figures. In the enveloping silence, her mind worked on its own, and she would begin to hear voices. On the cold floor was a beat-up mattress with stains and tears. No blanket, just a thin white sheet. If anyone or anything was on the ground, it could easily get to her.

It was so cold down there. A misty haze could be seen with every breath. The skin on her arms prickled with goosebumps. The tears that fell down her cheeks felt icy. The fear was petrifying.

Faith had been left in the basement for the night to repent for the sins she committed against her Lord that day at school. Her mother Evelyn told her that she needed to confront the darkness and trust in Jesus through the night. Her mother always told her that faith had to be tested. Faith had never actually spent a night in the scary basement before, but it was always mentioned, threatened. She never believed that her mother would cross the line and send her down there.

In the dark, she kept her eyes closed tightly. Usually, with all senses halted she could better feel an overwhelming sense of love in the presence of God whether it be during worship, during prayer, anywhere, or anytime. As long as you felt safe. But in the dark cold silence, in a locked basement, at midnight something different is felt when you close your eyes.

In the paralyzing presence of her fear, her mind was filled with dreadful thoughts. What if there were ghastly creatures down there, angered by her devotions and prayers, ready to attack her when she was at her most vulnerable? But she chastised herself. The fear of something attacking her in the basement should not speak louder than the voice of the Lord. It was a test to see if she believed she was safe enough to close her eyes. But even in high faith, she found with her eyes shut, she cried and shivered through her silent prayers for the rest of the night.

"Jesus, I pray that…" Faith's heart was beating so hard it felt like it could pop out of her chest. The second she closed her eyes, she imagined there was a demon an inch away from her face, smiling at her with its razor-sharp teeth.

She could literally feel the demon breathing on her neck, angry. Yet when she opened her eyes, there was nothing but darkness. "Father, I'm sorry that I…" There it was again, that feeling that stopped her dead in her tracks. It left her frozen with fear, contemplating a hundred negative thoughts per second. All she could think about was being attacked by a demon offended by her praise and love for Jesus Christ.

By some strange miracle, after hours spent in terror of the darkness both in the room and behind her eyes, she eventually worried herself into a deep sleep. There does come a point where a change has to be taken. To take a leap of faith and trust that you will wake up in the morning if you are brave enough to close your eyes.

Even asleep her busy mind wouldn't allow her to rest, and she was plagued by nightmares about the paranormal. In her dreams, she watched chairs skid from one end of the room to the other, dragged along the concrete floor by the hands of enraged ghosts. Restless, furious footsteps boomed and echoed all around her. Three knocks thundered from the walls. Three times to mock the Father, the Son, and the Holy Spirit.

"Wake up sweetheart."

Faith awoke to her mother looming over her body still huddled into a restless ball upon the mattress. Mama was a tall and slim woman, average in every way, unassuming to the casual glance. She blended in easily with all of the other mothers. The features of her face were conventional and yet at times frighteningly expressive. She had a fire in her eyes, stoked by her endless faith in God. The middle-aged woman's sense of style was plain, made up of simple jeans and t-shirts that were well-worn and faded with age. T-shirts that bore crosses and calligraphic scripture, adornments that reflected her love for God, which she wore with obvious pride.

It was a Saturday morning, so Mama was not at her office job today. She stood there above her daughter with an expression of genuine love on her face, warmth stamped soft into her features, framed by the light spilling in through the meager window.

"What time is it, Mama?" Faith asked as she began to slowly wake up.

"It is 8:30 sweetheart. I hope you got something out of the night."

The truth was, Faith had been too afraid of the unknown that had haunted her all night to even focus on what she did wrong at school. But if she told her mother that fear of the night had hindered her walk with God, her mother would make her spend another night in the basement. So though she felt conflicted about lying to her mother, she did.

"Mama, I repented last night and was able to find Jesus in the midst of all of my mess."

Evelyn gave a bright smile and, victoriously, quoted the scripture Colossians 3:23 to her daughter. "Whatever you do, do it with all your heart, as working for the Lord, not for human masters."

"Yes, Mama," said Faith in the sweetest tone of voice she could.

"We have to honor our Father through our work ethic, sweetheart. Does Getting a B on your English paper reflect the perfect image we are meant to emulate?" Her mother's tone was tender, but underlying it was familiar severity, a certain sternness nurtured by her rigid and relentless faith.

"No Mama, it doesn't," Faith replied with delicate earnestness, sincere though groggy from her fractured sleep, skin still tingling from the horrors of the night. "Jesus gave everything to me, so I should've studied more and given more of myself to him."

Evelyn looked at her daughter with pride and at last said, "Breakfast is ready, sweetheart."

This was something that happened pretty often when it came to Mama. The only one who seemed to be crazy about digging into things with Mama was their youngest sister. Faith and her older brother understood there was no winning against the will of their mother. Mama was the teacher and her children the students. As teacher, Mama's rules were strict and unforgiving, and any wrong answer could lead to something important being taken away like food or comfort, or even hours of spiritual disciplines. It was safer to just tell their mother what she wanted to hear.

Faith was the middle child of the modest Singleton family. At almost 13 years old, she was a demure and timid girl. Her mother dressed her plainly, denying her clothing that was deemed too flashy or too revealing. So Faith walked around in old hoodies and jeans as the other girls in the 8th grade wore bright colors and fashionable tops.

Faith felt like an outcast in school. It wasn't like she got picked on by the other kids, she was just ignored. There was nothing about her that stood out in either a good or a bad way. She was quiet and focused on her school work, which she excelled at. In fact, she had skipped the 7th grade entirely, and there was even talk that she might be pushed further into high school faster than the other kids. Though her mother dismissed this opportunity because she did not want her daughter to be exposed to life in high school so soon.

In the school library, Faith could avoid all of the other kids. Who amongst her peers would understand her? Who wanted to talk to a goodie-goodie church girl? Sure, some kids went to church, but Mama felt they were all misguided, and she would not let Faith become friends with these other children. Faith reminded herself, even when she was lonely, that she should be thankful to have a mother who was well immersed in the word of God. This was more important than having friends or fitting in.

In the past few years, Mama had taken Faith and her three siblings to many churches, all with hopes of being fed by sound doctrine. But, no pastor was good enough for Mama, who was quick to theological disagreements with both the pastors and their congregations.

Mama was brave and outspoken; she would puff up her chest, and say, "my children will not wait here and be led astray!" So the Singleton's had to leave many churches. Mama took it upon herself to teach the Singleton children the 'Way.' Together, they did daily Bible studies, devotions, and engaged in theological discussions. These sessions could last for hours if their mother was in the mood. Who needs church, Mama would ask them. Who needs a building full of broken people who have nothing but a false Gospel to teach?

One of the things that set Faith apart amongst the Singleton children was that she was adopted. She had no memory of her birth parents because Mama had raised her from a newborn. She was given no information about her birth parents or why they had given her up, but she was often reminded that she was just as much Mama's child as the others. Faith was a Singleton.

Still, Faith wrestled with the obvious question of who her parents were. She wanted to meet them someday and ask them why they did not want her. She wanted to look them both in the eye and demand to know why they gave up on her and how they could sleep at night knowing that someone else was raising their daughter? Faith wondered what they were like. Did they look like her? Did they share any of the talents or interests that she had? What kind of people were they in general? She often wondered what life would be like if she spent it with them. But she felt like a Singleton, and Evelyn felt like a real mother to her. But there was still a void that she wanted her birth parents to fill. Mama always told her that she would tell her more about them when she got older.

Ruth was the youngest of the children, nine years old and in the 4th grade. She had curly blonde hair that reached down to her shoulders and was also of simple taste in what she wore. In many ways, she wanted to be like her older sister. The child was already on her way to following in the footsteps of Faith's academic achievements, and she surpassed all of her peers in reading and mathematics. Even at the age of nine, Ruth displayed latent potential. She comprehended things on a level that could be considered almost genius. Her understanding of complex theology even surprised her family members. Ruth also had a strong faith in the Lord, and she felt no need to socialize with other kids. The innocent child held Mama up on a very high pedestal-- her mother was her hero.

The difference between her and Faith was that she appeared to be a far more expressive version of her sister. Her aggressive personality resembled that of Mama. Whereas Faith was ignored by her peers, Ruth was hated by the other kids and secretly by her teachers, too. She was too outspoken, especially for a nine-year-old. Everything that anybody said about anything was wrong. Because Ruth was naturally smarter than the other kids, they did not understand her most of the time. And because she was smarter than the other kids, Ruth did not want them to. She disliked people as much as they disliked her, and was very open about it. Rather than instruct her differently, Mama praised and rewarded Ruth. Those people of limited faith were below them.

But, Ruth knew how to play the system. She read her books, answered the questions, wrote her school papers in the proper format, and collected her A+ grades.

Another one of her siblings, James, was a year younger than Faith. He was a short boy with blonde messy hair, glasses, and plain clothing like the rest of his family. He was named after the book of James in the Bible. Mama felt there was a great deal of wisdom in this book, so she wanted to claim wisdom over James's life before it started. Ironically, unlike his two sisters and his older brother, James struggled academically.

James had a lot of trouble comprehending simple things. It took him hours to understand elementary concepts that other kids would grasp at first glance. He never understood the disconnect, though, or the blank thoughts that haunted his mind. Mama would not allow him to get the help he needed, either. She promised to never put him in a special class or educational program. Her reasons were Biblical. Moses told God that he was not good at speaking, but God still chose him for a very important task. So, to Mama, there was no excuse for James; there was no outside help needed by anyone but God. Mama felt that if Moses could lack but still be chosen by God, so too could James. And rather than seek to change his nature, he should embrace himself as God created, as surely he had a purpose for being as he was made. Yet, things were still frustrating for James because he wanted to be like his siblings and classmates.

James never asked himself what he thought of Mama. Was she right? Was she wrong? Rather than question her judgment, he decided to trust her guidance and took her word for it on all things. He went along with all of Mama's lessons. It wasn't necessarily that he didn't believe in anything, or that he was just trying to get by following the rules. No, he just felt too much of a disconnect in his thoughts to truly question his theological teachings.

James lived in his head. He often looked at other people and wondered what their life was like. Was their father gone too? Were they allowed to watch Saturday morning cartoons? Do they go to church? Quickly, those deep ponderings would be forgotten as something else caught his attention and pulled him out of his introspection. Perhaps a bird flying in the sky. And then his head would fill with distracting questions. What is it like to fly? Is it better to live by air and not inside a house? Does this bird live life carelessly or does it feel it is here for a reason?

James also was extremely socially awkward. He creeped people out. Nobody bullied him, though. Perhaps the other children didn't have it in them to bully someone who seemed so pathetic. He didn't make eye contact, and he isolated himself from the rest of the children at school. It was not uncommon to see James awkwardly eating his food alone or simply staring down at the floor.

Yet there were many things that James loved. He enjoyed movies, comic books, video games, and especially animals. He was often the one who would bring home a stray cat or puppy, which he would hide under his bed, hoping not to get caught. Of course, he would get caught every time and was made to let his rescued friends go. With animals, James was able to communicate in the way he should have been able to with his peers.

Then there was David. He was the oldest Singleton brother, 17 years old, and a senior in high school. He was tall and blonde, though his hair usually stayed buried inside of a beanie. Like his sisters, David was very intelligent. He took all honors classes and looked to graduating with many college credits. Unlike his sisters, he had lots of friends at school. David had an easy sort of personality that drew people in. There was an unnamable, undefinable, sort of charm in the young man that attracted people to him.

David hid it very well, but he was completely against his mother and all that she stood for. To be brutally honest, he hated her. It felt like an ugly and festering thing, this hate. Perhaps that was why he was so open and friendly to others. In some way, he compensated for the darkness that consumed his thoughts by projecting to others the mirror opposite. Regardless of his light manner, his friendly demeanor, he blamed Mama for his father leaving. It was her and her fervent religious beliefs that had pushed his father away five years ago.

All those years ago, his mother suffered frequent and intense breakdowns and paranoia. During these episodes, she would start fights with his father. David remembered long nights lying alone listening to the fighting and yelling happening just outside of his bedroom wall. Hollow and angry voices. Mama had a problem with everything his father did. She questioned everything: what he spent money on, what he ate for dinner, who his friends were, and when he worked. There was never a rational basis for any of her accusations. Once she got into the Bible and added religious belief to her paranoia, he just couldn't do it anymore. Evelyn said she was brought up on the Bible and lost her way when she got into a sinful relationship with his father, and now she was returning home.

To David, the Bible was all rubbish. It made absolutely no sense at all. He was to believe that an ancient book written by broken human beings, who were already religiously biased, contained the very words of God? A God who told him what he could and could not do? A supposedly loving God who would threaten His own creation with punishment as terrible as Hell. David felt that the book was fundamentally flawed and full of injustice. It encouraged women not to speak in church, and that's sexist. It does not take a stand against slavery. In fact, it encouraged slaves to obey their masters through fear of the Lord. Not to mention, God in physical form was nowhere to be seen when you call on his name for prayer.

It all just made David very annoyed. The fact that these lessons were being forced upon him by the woman he hated most made him even more resentful. But he was not one to crush beliefs or ruin children's dreams. He could not win an argument with his mother, and he did not want to face any repercussions for expressing his doubts and criticisms. So David played along for his brother and sisters' sakes, for Mother's sake, and of course, for his own sake. His family all believed David was as much of a believer or more. As the man of the house, it was up to David to set an example for his siblings. But deep down, he couldn't wait to graduate and live on a college campus. He dreamed of leaving his crazy life behind.

David was 12 when their father left. The other siblings were too young to fully understand what had happened. They were all in love with Mama then. David had some sense of right and wrong even as a young child, so he understood what was happening as his parents' relationship unraveled. But as younger children, the siblings always defended Mama. They were unable to place themselves in the shoes of their father, which was expected for children of their age. This was just life to them. Mama was good and Father was bad. Mama ran the household, though, and she was always the biggest personality among the two.

David missed his father. Back then, he had been his father's pride and joy. David had memories as clear as a crystal of throwing a baseball back and forth with his father in the front yard. It seemed like forever ago, and life was much simpler then. He remembered the love his father showed him. And his father had a gentle soul, which made him no match for Mama's spirit and passion. Or her anger.

No one who knew both his father and mother understood how and why the two of them had ended up together. After all, their very natures were polar opposites-- his father was compassionate while Mama was abrasive. Even when she was wrong, which was most of the time, Mama was great at arguing. Father would be easily backed into a corner about anything and everything Mama had a problem with, even when he was right. Watching his parent's fight had made young David terribly afraid of the torrential force that was Mama. The memories of his formative years were fraught with violence and venom. At her most angry, Mama would throw dishes at his father, break his possessions, and beat him up with flurries of punches and kicks. It was a regular routine to be woken up in the middle of the night by their screaming.

Deep down, David had hoped his father would escape, leave for good, and take him away. But when his father left, he left David behind.

It was a dreary night when David found his mother crying on the living room floor. "Mama, what's wrong?" he had asked.

David remembered how she had looked up at him with thick tears in her eyes and said, "Your father left a few hours ago. He is not coming back to us. He does not want to be a family!"

David recalled falling to the floor and sobbing uncontrollably, consumed by a confused ache that begged to know how his father could have discarded him. All of a sudden, he had felt terribly lonely, worthless. "Why would he just leave without saying goodbye? What happened?"

Mama reached out, tender for once, and embraced her child. "He could not handle the responsibility of being a husband and father. He was not able to put us before himself. Your father is not a real man!"

David began to hate his father then, a hatred that was further nurtured by his deep feeling of abandonment. Of course, he also hated Mama because she was the one who drove his father away. But she was right about what she said. Father was no real man.

"Baby, you need to hold your head high," Mama instructed. "Baby, you are named after a great King. There are power and leadership in your name. You will grow up and become the man your father never was. I will protect you and you will grow up to become the man of the house."

One of the things that frustrated David the most was that he had to do everything without the guidance of his father. Watching his friends with their fathers had made him feel bitter and cold. Nonetheless, he learned how to shave on his own, a very bloody and dramatic affair. When it came time for David to learn to drive, he relied on the lessons of his teacher and neighbor. Despite the many hardships, David was proud of his accomplishments, made all the more fruitful and gratifying because he had done it all on his own. And now, here he was about to graduate High School and move on to college.

David held onto the memory of his father leaving as tight as he could. Lying awake at night, David often visualized the moment he would see his father again face to face. He would look at his old man in the face and tell him, "Yeah, I did it all without your help." His strength was often a front for how unloved he felt.

And David was always aware that he was different from his siblings. He was an Atheist in a Christian household. No good would ever come of telling his siblings that everything they believed about God was lies. Even an atheist such as David had to admit that their Bible studies had made them good, moral children.

He did not agree with Mama putting Faith in the basement with the door locked, yet there was nothing that he could do. David consoled the ache of his helplessness by telling himself that Faith was not being physically harmed. She was not being beaten. Maybe he had to tell himself that purely because he couldn't help Faith no matter how badly he wanted. Even as the man of the house, David had no power over Mama. On some basic level, David felt like he was failing at his duty, and certainly failing his siblings.

So what if Mama didn't want his sisters to wear certain name brands. If they couldn't have sleepovers, couldn't listen to certain music, or watch certain movies. David went behind his mother's back and did what he wanted. No one was getting hurt, though he understood that there would be severe repercussions should his extracurricular activities be discovered. It was well worth it to feel like he had some freedom, some free will. For David, secrets were easy to keep. After all, he spent half his life hiding what Mama did behind closed doors.

Soon, he told himself. *Soon you will leave for college and never look back.*

There would be no more fighting or fear. No more lies.

***

Faith began to walk up the steep stairs of the basement, back into the brightly lit hallway lined with photographs that hinted at a happy, normal life. Ugly truths were hidden in those innocent smiles.

She worked her way into the kitchen to find her brother's and sister already all together seated at the table. David was trying to hide a look of both disgust and pity, not happy about his little sister spending the night in a dark basement.

Where all of the Singleton children could see and hear, Mama asked Faith if she had learned her lesson.

"Of course I did," the girl replied as genuinely as she could.

Mama had gone all-out making breakfast, and Faith was starving from her night in the foreboding basement. There was pancakes, bacon, sausage, toast with butter and jelly, and chocolate milk. There was a look on Mama's face of happiness and excitement as she told them to "dig in." But, of course, not before they said their prayer.

As they ate large portions of sweet and greasy food, Mama began her speech. "There is something I want you kids to learn through this perfectly cooked breakfast, so listen well." Mama smiled and calmly continued to speak as she poured chocolate milk into her glass. "I put my all into this breakfast. I woke up bright and early, I made extra portions, and I even got chocolate milk instead of regular milk. I want this breakfast to reflect the image of my Lord and Savior, and he is perfect. He gave everything to me; he gave himself to me when he died on the cross. Because of this, I have to give all of myself in everything I do. That includes this breakfast I made for you guys this morning."

David's reaction was cynical-- if Mama wanted to reflect the perfect image of the Lord, why did she not do so every day? James ate his pancakes with a blank expression, while Faith listened quietly but with intent. Ruth hung onto every word.

"There should be something inside of you that pushes you to reflect God's glory," Mama continued, "Faith, Jesus was not a B+ when he patiently waited to perform his first miracle. He was not a B+ when he embarked on a ministry to spread the message of his Father. He was not a B+ when he followed truth and purpose into persecution. He was not a B+ when he had the flesh ripped off of him, and he humbled himself to die on a cross. He was not a B+ when he forgave his transgressors for torturing and murdering him in cold blood."

The kitchen grew silent. Looks of guilt and contemplation passed over the faces of James and his sisters. David had so much he wanted to say, but he held his tongue. Mama's expression was utterly calm, but her eyes were hard and serious. She paused for a few seconds to give them a few seconds to think about what she said. Then at last she took a deep breath and released a soft sigh. "He was an A+ when his plan and purpose became a reality on the third day."

Everyone at the table began to clap and smile, except David, who could only plaster upon his face a fake, empty smile. Nobody noticed it because they were so wrapped up in Mama's great lesson.

David felt sick to his stomach, and the heavy food that settled in it turned over. The utter insanity of the moment struck him with abrupt clarity. He honestly couldn't wrap his mind around how his siblings could even buy this. Who talks like this? It's not normal. Who forces hourly Bible studies on their children? Who punishes a child for a B+? Who sends their child into a dark cold basement for the night? He felt disgusted by Mama because she was a walking contradiction. She could preach love for one moment, then lock her daughter in a dirty basement for the next moment.

Still, he was happy that his younger siblings hadn't witnessed his version of Evelyn. She got better once she started taking medication. In all honesty, David was very surprised that she had accepted the diagnosis of her psychiatrist. Even medicated, she was still not all there upstairs, but it did bring a sort of balance to her life. It kept her from having violent outbursts, and she had more and more moments where she was *nice* to them. But it was still obvious that she was crazy, and it was only a matter of time before someone else started to think for themselves as David had.

"Can I be excused," asked James. Mama asked him why, and he told her that he was done with breakfast and wanted to go for a walk around the neighborhood.

Mama paused to think about her answer and said, "Sure honey, and try to get some prayer time in while you're walking around."

James awkwardly shook his head in a yes motion and made his way outside.

Ruth happily ate her food and began to tell Mama all about the prayer journal that she was starting to put together. For a child her age, it was amazing how organized she was. Mama was happy as ever to hear the news that her youngest had her own prayer journal as Mama had many of her own. Mama's example was what motivated Ruth to work through her first journal so she could do more of them. All the child really wanted to do was make her mother proud of her.

"Faith, sweetheart, I pray you are not angry with me for where I sent you. I just want you to be strong in the Lord. I wanted you to confront where you went wrong and to find Christ."

Faith looked up at Mama and asked her a question, "What did I tell you this morning Mama?"

Mama smiled and said, "You repented and found Jesus."

Ruth enthusiastically jumped out of her chair and hugged her sister tight. "I am so happy for you Faith!"

"Thank you, Ruth," Faith said as she continued to finish her breakfast.

Chapter 2
Happy Birthday

A week later, James was excited about his 12th birthday. What made the day even better was that it happened to fall on a Saturday that year. He didn't have to worry about going to school that day or the next, so it was like having a birthday that lasted two days. He could wake up Sunday morning, enjoy a piece of leftover birthday cake, and spend time enjoying the presents he received.

Mama told him last night that she had something really special for him on his birthday. All he had to do was patiently wait the day out. Whatever she had for him was going to happen at 7 p.m. that Saturday night.

Of course, religious-based things were the center of life in the Singleton household, but Mama didn't think everything was evil. Spiderman, Batman, and other superheroes were not banned. Certain video games were allowed if they weren't rated M for Mature. The children could watch whatever they wanted as long as it wasn't drenched in curse words and all the other content that comes with R- rated films. The Singleton children were able to do anything they wanted after their daily devotionals were done.

With that being said, James loved superhero movies, and he loved video games.

Last year for his birthday, he was given the original Spiderman movie collection. In his possession, at last, were the original 3 films that Tobey Maguire starred in. James felt people did not appreciate the actor enough as the perfect Spiderman, so it was a big deal for him to own the movies.

Mama had a way of turning superhero moments into God moments. On the part of the first Spiderman movie when Uncle Ben tells Peter, "with great power, comes great responsibility," Mama kept saying, "yes Jesus." She saw Jesus all over that quote. She always pressed upon her children to see God in everything they could because God was in everything. All the Marvel superhero movies would get turned into deep messages from Mama. It was just something James had grown to accept, and he didn't ponder the messages too deeply. He was only an 12-year-old boy who saw Spiderman.

If there was one thing James would change about his birthdays, it was to have a real party with friends and family. Most of his family avoided them because of Mama. His grandparents lived in Washington State where Mama was born. All uncles, cousins, and aunts never came around, and the Singletons did not go and visit them either. Life has always been Mama and them, and their father too for the few years he was around. His distant family nonetheless sent him bright cards full of money, which James loved a lot.

He was not an academic achiever. He got lost easily in his head, lost in any world that was not the real world. When he watched a movie, he was the sort of kid who wanted to be the characters in the movie. He saw himself in the Spiderman suit. He saw himself hiding his identity in the Batcave. He imagined himself the one who was most important, the bravest and strongest, the one who overcomes when all seems lost and hopeless.

Like he got lost in movies, he also found himself lost in music. He was the guy singing songs in his head, imagining there was a giant crowd enjoying every moment. When he drew in his sketchbook, he was cut off from the very room around him. Perhaps he wanted to be disconnected because in these separate worlds he was happy and free to be himself.

James waited with excited, bubbling anticipation for 7 p.m. to come. He had devised a plan the night before to reduce the time he had to wait for his big surprise. The plan was to stay up as late as he could the previous night by watching movies, playing his race car games, and drawing superheroes of his own creation. By his childish logic, if he was able to fall asleep past 3 a.m., he would wake up at 4 p.m. or later. That would leave only three hours until his great surprise. It was a perfect and flawless plan, but it had that Christmas Eve effect on him. The one where you are too excited to fall asleep, and you keep waking up because your mind is running a million miles a minute. James managed to stay awake until 6 a.m., but the excitement over his birthday surprise was too much. He woke up after only three hours of sleep and couldn't go back to bed.

"Children, we are going to get into our time with God now!" Mama yelled enthusiastically so the entire house could hear her. "You know how it is, we hear from God first, then we go on with our day. You have an hour, then I want us all to talk about what you have read and heard."

This was an every morning thing for the Singletons: wake up early, read the Bible, pray on what you read, find the application - how it applies to your life-, then meet up and share with each other what each had learned.

This was not much of an issue for anyone except David, who just mostly pretended to go along with the reading and contemplation.

The thing that upset the children from time to time was when they had to study beyond the morning devotion. There were many ways to earn additional study time. For example, talking back meant more time in the word. Arguing with your brother or sister, more time in the word. Disagreeing with Mama on what the passages meant, more time in the word.

This was why the children never tried to question things too much. Everybody agreed with Mama's interpretation of the scriptures, and that kept her happy. But it was obvious that Ruth genuinely agreed with everything that she read, and that Mama said. She was always the one who had the most to say when they shared. David was the one who said the most interesting things about what he read. He honestly just knew what to say. It was no different than his reading assignments at school: read a passage or book and write a paper about it. Faith was quiet, sweet, and had a gentle tone of voice when she discussed. She would agree with the passages of scripture and the way Mama interpreted them, but she was not as passionate as Ruth was about the material. James just found simple things to say, agreeing when he felt it would bail him out of too many deep conversations so that he could get on with his day.

Ruth had just finished reading part of the Gospel where Jesus performed his first miracle at the wedding, turning water into wine. The child closed her eyes and asked God to show her what he wanted her to understand from this passage. It was not long before she opened her eyes in a rush of excitement and began skipping happily down the hallway. Her shoes made tiny little squeaks on the hardwood floor as she pranced her way down the hall. On her way, she passed the bathroom where Mama stood holding the orange bottles that contained her daily prescription doses. She must have just run out of her medicine because the bottles were empty. She told her they kept her sharp and helped her go on with her day as a normal person would. When Ruth was seven years old, while playing absently with her toys, she asked Mama about the pills.

"Honey, the doctor gave them to me because they help my mind stay sharp. They keep my mind in order, they keep me from being sad, and I am able to go on with my day like anyone else," Mama told her, placing each bottle into the medicine cabinet one at a time before shutting it softly.

Ruth was too young to understand what Mama meant by all of that, so she pondered in her little head for a moment before turning back to her mother with a new inquiry: "Why did the doctor give you orange bottles and not other people?" Ruth didn't have any orange bottles, and she knew that none of her siblings did either.

Mama smiled gracefully and replied, "Some people are tested a little bit more. They battle things that are hard to fight on their own, and God made doctors who are smart enough to help people like Mama."

At that, Ruth smiled and hugged her Mama, and then ran back to her dolls.

While Ruth studied dutifully that morning, Faith was lost in her thoughts. Faith knew she needed to be reading her Bible, but she could not stop thinking of the basement. Mama had never done something that extreme before. Surely Mama knew the strength of the punishment she bestowed because she knew Faith was afraid of the dark. Had Mama forgotten? Did she not remember the time they played hide and seek together and Faith hid in the basement? Mama accidentally locked her in and left her there for an hour that felt like forever to Faith. She had been utterly terrified. Faith cried and banged on the door until Mama at last opened the door.

Faith knew Mama loved her, she knew that Mama meant well, but she just couldn't help feeling that what Mama had done to her was cruel.

Sometimes it was hard for Faith to have the deep connections with God that she wanted to have. Mama told her that her bond with God should be strong, flawless, and Faith doubted if she was capable. She never read the Bible out of her own desire. It was just a part of her daily routine, part of a checklist for the day. This was how she was raised, and it was all she knew. For the Singleton children, reading the Bible every morning was no different than having to brush their teeth or wash their faces. She said her prayers at night, and she did have moments where she reflected over the things she read, but it was not like Mama.

Faith had moments where she couldn't help but wonder if the absence of her birth parents was a reflection of her connection to her heavenly Parent. After all, Ruth had her mother in plain sight every day. Her birth mother was there reading the Bible, praying, walking out her faith, being an example to follow.

Mama said she grew up a believer, but she lost her way during her marriage with their father, John Singleton. As Mama told the story, she had an encounter with Jesus a few years after the start of her marriage, and it changed her forever. There was an undeniable love and excitement in Mama when she dug into the Bible. Most people understood the idea of being raised in this truth, of going to church or Sunday School. But it was always obvious that Mama was a lot stronger in her walk with Jesus. Ruth was a Mama's girl and took after her. James went with the flow, but he lived in his head. David was the big brother who was wise in every word he said. He was the rock. The one that held everything together. He was the one that brought love and encouragement when his siblings felt defeated or lost.

"Hey Faith, what's up," said David as he slowly entered her room with a look of genuine care.

"Not much. Trying to think of where to start in this book." She looked up for a moment as she turned the thin pages of her personal Bible, hoping that what David saw in her eyes was clarity and not fear.

"Gotcha. Look, Faith, are you okay?"

She had an idea why he was asking her this but still responded, "Yeah, why wouldn't I be?"

David's facial expression changed. Something behind his eyes made Faith think that there was something David wanted to say, something that he struggled with, but could not verbalize. Finally, his look lightened and became that of a simple and concerned older brother, "You spent the night locked in a dark basement. I just want to make sure you are okay."

Faith, still shaken by the night before, took a deep breath and replied, "Thank you for always taking care of me, David, but I promise that I am okay. It was scary, but I really did experience God while I was down there."

He looked back at her with a pause, eyes narrowing just a bit in silent questioning, studying her face to see signs of a lie. Faith felt on edge because she loved her brother, but she did not want him to force her to confront things that she would rather leave in the night. Finally, a smile lit up his features.

"Okay, sis. Well, you should probably just pick a random sentence in any scripture and just run with it. Just pull the whole, 'I felt super drawn to this one short passage because....' bit."

Faith and David both began to laugh with each other. For a few short moments, the events of the night before vanished from Faith's heart, and she felt light again. Safe. David was always so warm and so comforting. The two siblings huddled in close to each other, keeping their laughter contained or else Mama might hear and know that they were not at their lessons.

When their laughter died down, David placed a hand on her shoulder and squeezed. "Hurry up, Mama won't let us do anything today if we don't get through these devotions."

Sometimes, it nearly killed David not to be honest with Faith about how he felt. He couldn't tell if he was a good person for allowing her to hold onto a faith that was helping her, or if he was a bad person for allowing her to hold onto a faith that may very well not be real. He felt like an imposter when he answered her spiritual questions; he felt like he was lying to her every time he did it. There were often moments when he wanted to tell her how crazy all of it sounded. Nobody should have to do this, be forced to study the Bible. Nobody should have to fear punishment when it comes to spirituality.

But David just couldn't find it within himself to step up and say anything about it to Faith. This was one of the reasons he enjoyed quality time with his socially awkward little brother James. That kid just wanted to play video games or watch a movie. There was no deep spiritual talk between the two of them.

David was leaving Faith's bedroom and making his way through the hallway when he heard Mama call out to him, "David, can you come here please?"

He paused, not thinking much of it, and followed his mother's voice into her bedroom. Her bedroom was full of religious-themed decorations: crosses, portraits of Jesus, well-decorated hunks of wood with scripture engraved in cursive, and a giant bed against the wall. As Evelyn did her makeup in the mirror of her dresser, she began to speak.

"So David, I want to share something with you. Something very exciting."

He had no idea what this could mean, but tried to sound as positive and supportive as he could. "Well, what is it?"

She smiled and began to speak, "Last week, I feel like Jesus gave me healing from whatever the doctor says I have. Whatever ailment He had given me to take those prescription pills for all these years is now gone. I stopped taking them. I flushed them all, and I can hear his voice more clearly now."

David was always one to not say anything, but he just couldn't play along this time. "Mama, please don't take this the wrong way, but are you sure that was a good idea? I remember what it was like before you started taking them. I just don't want that to happen again."

She looked back on him with genuine love and said, "I know it was hard. Your father was not perfect and neither was I. It is true that I didn't have these pills to calm me down at the time, but I also didn't have Jesus. Not until the end, when it was too late."

He couldn't help thinking that made it so much worse.

Things didn't get better until she saw a doctor and began taking those pills. Sure, religion was not David's thing, but it was better than the constant screaming. It was much better than the dramatic episodes that took place every day before. But David was sincerely happy that his mother was happy. Not because he loved her, but because life was just easier that way.

"I was 8-years-old when you grabbed me by the ankles and dragged me around the house. When Dad made you mad and he went to work. You barged in my bedroom while I was playing and you took everything out on me. I was screaming and crying, and I got a rug burn. We cannot go back to that!"

Evelyn paused, a look of pure shock struck her face. At last, she took a breath and said, "I know I hurt you. I know it was a nightmare, and you have no idea how much guilt I carry for the way I treated you. I have had a lot of talks with my Savior about it. I have confronted my behavior before his throne, at his very feet, a thousand times. I just want to feel closer to him. I want to hear his voice."

Her eyes brimmed with tears, sadness stamped upon her every feature, and her body began to shiver. It was evident that all she wanted was to feel closer to the one who made her happy. Who wouldn't want more of what appeared to be working? But David knew this was not good for her. It was breaking him just as much as it was breaking her. This was a decision that would surely make life at home a complete hell. Before, his siblings were too young to remember, but now they would suffer.

"Mom, what makes you think you can't hear him while you are on the pills? What is the difference? They have helped you a lot." A look of worry was beginning to darken over his positive expression. Pure worry took hold of his tone of voice.

"Honey, that is the point. I should not have to lean on these pills to hear the voice of my Lord. A silent whisper told me I would hear him more if I flushed them all. It challenged my faith. I had to ask myself if I believed there was more power in his name than in the inside of a pill bottle. I know it was him because his voice is heard in the silence, not the loud thunder."

He stood there frozen, looking at his mother with a feeling of defeat, trying to think of something on the spot, anything that would make her reconsider her decision. Something that would not offend her, or make her suspect he lacked faith in her God. "Mom, God created the doctors. He gifted them accordingly to make medicine, so this is God helping you. It's okay to take the medicine."

"I can't honey. I have my mind made up. I know this is a good thing-"

"Mom," David interrupted. "Even Moses was given a staff to do the work of his Father. He used this gift from God to perform miracles. It was the very instrument that set the Israelites free from captivity. It brought the Pharaoh down to his knees. It set a plague on the Egyptians! God equips us with the tools we need to do his work. For you, it's to take these pills!"

David shifted gradually from concerned to angry. He was starting to find it difficult to hide the fact he felt so wrong about this. For the first time, he was about to engage in an actual argument with her. He would let her know that he was not following her the way his brother and sisters were.

In a serious but calm tone of voice, he asked her a question that could potentially lead to something very bad. "Mom, I need you to tell me something."

"What is it?" Her tone of voice was starting to go from loving and kind to irritated.

"Did you flush your pills before or after you locked Faith in the basement?"

The atmosphere changed at that very moment. The tension between the two practically screamed. Speechless. David even started to question if engaging in this conversation was worth it. Would any good come out of it? Was it ever possible to change her mind?

Evelyn looked like she was struggling to keep her motherly facial expression. She was finding it harder to sound sweet and gentle like she has been. She was starting to feel angry. Irritable. In awe that her son would even ask her something like this. He clearly didn't have faith in her. She knew what she was talking about, she knew God wanted her to do this.

It made her remember Matthew 16:23, when Jesus tells Peter, *"Get behind me Satan!"* A moment where Peter tried to talk Jesus out of something he felt called to do. But she quickly composed herself, and she allowed that look of motherly love and care to take over her face and tone of voice. When she could speak again, she said, "I think it's time for us to go over what we read in God's word this morning. I know this is scary. I am empathetic. I understand more than you probably know. But baby, everything is going to be just fine. I am better without them, and better with Him. I am excited to hear what you have to say this morning. You always have a way of bringing the best out of what you read."

The atmosphere began to return back to what it was before. It was calm, normal, and no more tension seemed to be felt in the air. This was his way out, he could walk away without digging himself in a hole. So David just looked at his mother and nodded.

"Yeah, you're right. I'm sorry Mom. I am not trying to doubt you."

"Well let's get started then," she said with her sweet positive tone back in place.

***

It was another Saturday breakfast for the Singleton family. They ate cereal and discussed what they felt from their devotions. Faith took David's advice and just took one random line and drug it out into a deeper meaning. Mama ate it up. She was just happy to see her children hearing from God. James tried to say a little bit more with hopes that it would bring a better outcome for his birthday. Ruth felt the need to top the dragged out word that her sister gave. She went on and on about timing. How Jesus was not ready to perform his miracle yet, that he felt the timing was not right. She took that and ran with it.

"We have to be intentional with not only what and how we do things, but when." Ruth was feeling very proud of herself. Mama chimed in and made sure to mention that it was Jesus's mother who told her son it was time. "I guess Mama always knows best." Chuckles started to make its way around the table.

Then David began to speak on the concept of predestination. This was the idea that God had predestined everything before the beginning of time. This was one of David's biggest problems with God. If God knew what's going to happen before it happened, then why allow certain things to happen at all? David often thought about the concept of predestination alongside that of Heaven and Hell. If everything is predetermined, then God knows who is destined for Hell before they are even born. And, if God is loving, why would he allow humans to waste their life on Earth just to meet a bitter fate in the end? It made no sense to David.

But being the good son and brother he was, he said, "The mysteries of God are so amazing. He is so powerful and unfathomable. He is able to find a way for free will and predestination to co-exist without negatively affecting each other."

Everyone at the table was mesmerized and impressed by his insight.

After breakfast, James decided to take a walk around his neighborhood. It was only noon, and this meant he still had to wait seven more hours until his big surprise. As he walked around his neighborhood, he was able to see the long rows of houses on either side of him stretch to the horizon, each made of bright colors with neatly kept lawns. It seemed like there were groups of kids playing with each other every few houses down. A group of older kids crossed paths with him, and James wondered, *"Maybe they are all about to go kill some time at the gas station at the end of the street."*

It occurred to him that he was alone. Yet, he wasn't sad about being alone, he just wondered if it was a bad thing to always be alone. What did it mean for him to walk down the street by himself? To not have a group of friends on his front lawn? Why did nobody ever try to talk to him at school? Why did nobody ever try to bully him at school? An even better question, why didn't he try to make friends? Was he a loser for having no friends to invite to his house for his birthday

As he walked along the sidewalk, he pondered what his mother could have possibly gotten for him. Lost in his thoughts, James navigated the familiar streets of his neighborhood until he came to a path that led into the woods. Normally, he would cut through someone's yard and explore the woods behind the houses. Sometimes, he would be able to see someone else's life through the outside of their windows. Shrouded by the heavy branches of dense trees, nobody ever knew he was watching.

There was one house in particular that James found himself returning to several times a week. From his secret place along the fringe of the woods, he had a perfect view into one of the house's upstairs bedroom windows.

The reason why he liked to watch this house was because of an older high school girl named Sarah. He found her breathtaking, and to him, she looked like a goddess. He often visualized himself being with someone as beautiful as her someday, and the sight of her would set his heart racing. Sometimes, James would even wait minutes, hours, just to see her for a mere few seconds in the frame of her window.

Once again, he found himself in that spot. James searched the ground until he found a broken tree trunk on the ground large enough to be used as a place to sit. He looked up and to his convenience, Sarah's bedroom window was open. The timing was absolutely perfect because at that moment she walked around her room, crossing the window every few seconds.

As James watched her, he wondered like he often did what was going on in her life. What she was doing that day? Was she happy or sad? What did her room actually look like beyond the window? Would she ever talk to him? As his head filled with questions, his mind wandered off into deep thought, only to be shocked back to reality when he realized that Sarah was about to change her shirt.

His eyes grew big in his head, wider than he thought possible, and he felt his heart start to beat harder and faster. She had on a pink bra, and her skin looked smooth. To him, she not only looked like a goddess, but she was exotic. Sarah looked more beautiful than any woman he'd ever seen before; more beautiful than any actress or pop star. It was suddenly hard to breathe as his breath came from his parted lips faster, and all he could think about was how he needed to see more of her.

She paused and stood in plain view at her bedroom window. For a few seconds, she stared off into space. With every heavy heartbeat, James sat mesmerized, thinking to himself, *"Please show more."*

But it was then that something very strange occurred. Sarah suddenly looked out of the window in his direction, and his worst fear happened. She looked directly at him. Frozen where he sat, all James could do was stare back at her with a blush blooming on his face. Finally, after an agonizing wait, she smiled at him, winked, and waved.

At that very moment, his heart burst into a million pieces, and fear, at last, took over his body. Mobilized, he jumped off of the tree trunk and ran away as quickly as he could. Once he was as far away as possible, he found himself thinking a bittersweet thought. This may be the last time he would ever see Sarah, but he was still happy he got to see her today, even if he did get caught.

He took a deep breath and kept his body moving, circling around the block. His walk took him about an hour, and he returned home just around one o'clock.

Mama handed him a stack of mail when he returned home. His grandparents, aunt, and uncle all gave him money, and some other distant relatives had sent some, as well. James was happy to have pocketed over 100 dollars. He asked his mom if she could drive him to the store to buy some movies, and to his excitement, she told him to wait for his surprise first. Five and a half hours were left, that was all. This felt like an eternity for James.

***

Meanwhile, Ruth was sitting on the floor reading her Bible and writing in her pink prayer journal. She wanted to make Mama proud, so she tried to stay on top of her daily reflections. There was something about that feeling, the feeling of being accepted. Hearing things like "good job" and "I'm so proud" from Mama made her feel warm inside. Ruth thrived off of that simple feeling. There was not much thought as to why she wanted to feel this all the time, she just thought about how she could feel it often.

She loved the moments when she bonded with Mama, sitting on opposite ends of her giant bed, talking about the Bible. Ruth cherished it all: the sweet tone in Mama's voice, the patience she had with Ruth's many questions, the wise and considerate answers she gave, but most importantly, the presence of love. It felt good to be held close, taken care of, guided, and loved. So, Ruth chased that feeling. Pretty soon, she would complete her second devotional of the day and report it to her mother in her bedroom. Then she would be able to feel the wonderful feelings all over again.

To her surprise, Mama walked into her bedroom, proud to find Ruth on her own at her devotions. "Baby, this brings me so much joy. It never fails. Every time I see you at such a young age, clinging to his word."

The child smiled back at Mama and gave a tight hug. "I love ya."

"I love you too, sweetheart. So anyway, I have to go to the grocery store for a couple of things, and I could use some company. Would you like to go?"

Ruth was overwhelmed and overjoyed at the idea of spending her day with Mama, just the two of them, where Ruth did not have to share Mama's attention or vie for it among her siblings. This was perfect. "Of course Mama let's go!"

Within half an hour, Ruth and Mama took off in the white Town and Country van. As Mama drove, Ruth told her everything she had picked up on in her second devotion. Just like every other time, she was given the response and praise she was hoping for. Once again, Ruth was the little daughter that made Mama so proud.

Ruth floated on a cloud the entire way through the grocery store, obediently collecting items and placing them in the rickety metal cart until they had all that they needed, paid, and started to head back home.

On the way out of the parking lot, they saw a homeless man asking for change on the patch of grass next to the red stoplight. Without any hesitation, Mama pulled 20 dollars out of her purse and gave it to the man.

"That was really nice of you, Mama."

Mama looked back at her daughter and smiled, "You know that what we do to the least of these, we do to Jesus."

"Yeah, Mama." The girl couldn't be any happier to have a mother that was not only loving to her, but to the stranger on the side of the street.

***

David went out with his friends around midday. He did not spend as much time at home as his brother and sisters, but then he had a lot more freedom at his age. He had a part-time job at the movie theater, as well. Honestly, David only worked there to earn a little money to hang out with his friends. In addition to his friends and job, he had his old 1991 Camry that his mother bought him last year for his birthday.

It was not much, but it helped him get away.

Faith was stuck in a new book that she had checked out from the school library. The girl sat there utterly absorbed in it, but this was normal for her. She often spent most of her time reading, and she would read anything and everything.

To pass the hours after he returned from his walk, James watched Batman movies, eyes darting to the clock every few minutes in anticipation of 7 p.m. Ruth watched TV in the living room once she returned home from shopping.

Because time was not always cruel, 7 p.m. came eventually. Mama showed up in James's room before he could go look for her himself. She smiled and said, "I hope you don't think I forgot about you."

"Of course not, Mama." He could not contain his excitement, and he leaped to his feet ready to follow his mother.

"Okay, honey, follow me," she said.

With utter trust and no hesitation, James followed her into the living room.

Mama called both Ruth and Faith into the room, as well, and instructed them to sit on the couch together. "So as we all know, today is your brother's birthday. He is 12 years old today."

Both Faith and Ruth started to cheer and hug their brother.

"I spent a lot of time trying to figure out how to make this birthday special," Mama continued. "I even prayed about it. With lots of prayer, Jesus spoke to me, and I was able to come up with an idea of how to make this birthday extra special for James."

The boy was elated and excited, mind alive with every possibility as to what she could have bought him? Did she buy him all the movies he wanted? Was she going to let him play a game he was not mature enough to play? What the heck did she get him? His sisters even looked interested in what it could be.

With a gentle smile and a pause for effect, Mama continued, "Last year I spent 100 dollars on your birthday. The joy that came across your face was worth every penny. If there is anything that makes me happy, it is seeing that look on your face. I was praying to Jesus all last week, asking him what to do for you this year. He answered me... James, I did not get you anything for your birthday."

James couldn't believe what he just heard. He felt very confused and also wondered if this was all some joke.

She continued, "When we die, we cannot take material things to the grave with us. None of that matters. We are so attached to material things, and Jesus said this is not our home. The word says not to get too attached, that love for the world will make you an enemy of God."

As Mama talked, James couldn't help but feel heartbroken. Like someone had reached into his body and taken a handful of oxygen from him. He fought to hold back his cresting tears. This was all a little boy could think about all day, and his disappointment threatened to crush him. In a heartbroken way, he finally started to accept it. Mama really didn't get him anything for his birthday.

"I feel like a lesson to take with you to your grave is a far better gift than one I can put a price on. I actually took the 100 dollars I would've spent on you today and gave it to a child who was poor. Well, gave it to his mother, who was upset she couldn't get him anything for his birthday. I just felt like this year would be one to give and not receive. But you are really receiving so much more. What we do for the least of these, we do for Jesus."

James did not at first notice it when it happened, but he had tears falling down his cheeks. He was devastated, confused, and not prepared for this.

Mama looked at her son with an expression of genuine care mixed with disappointment in him for his tears. "Honey, do not be this way. Rejoice. This is a good thing. Do not let yourself become selfish. Do not give the Lord any reason to need repentance from you. I thought you would be a little more excited about this."

Even his sisters on the couch had very confused looks on their faces. It was evident in the looks that they shot him, but they felt terrible for him.

James was full of a conflict that he was too young to understand or reconcile. On one hand, he was glad to know that some needy child had their wishes come true for once in their life. Yet, on the other hand, he was terribly let down and sullen. The boy desperately wanted to pull himself together, but he was too saddened. All day he had walked in hopeful clouds, and now he had been harshly sent back down to Earth.

In a tone of voice that resembled that of a young boy who just had his heart crushed, he found the strength to tell his mom, "Thank you."

She looked back at him gracefully and gave him the okay to head back into his room.

As James turned sadly around and started to make his way toward his bedroom, Mama asked, "James, you are forgetting something?"

He paused with no clue of what it could be and looked back at her.

"Baby, you still have something that belongs to someone who needs it more."

He was not ready for this. He had no idea what she was talking about, but he knew he was not going to like it.

"The 100 dollars that you got in the mail today, I need you to give it to me," Mama said.

James and his sisters shared awestruck expressions with each other. None of them could believe what was happening. But it *was* happening.

After a pause to gain his bearings, James sighed very softly and reached his hand into his pocket. Out of it he pulled all of his birthday money, clutched in his fist as if to not let it go. Tears fell steadily down his face, his hands shook, and his nerves strained, unable to handle the disappointment. But still, he walked over to his mother and gave her the money.

"Happy Birthday, sweetheart. I am so proud of you." She paused and took a breath, smiling because she truly felt that she got a very important point across to her children tonight. "Well, I guess you guys can go back to your rooms now."

The rest of the day was very sad and dreary for everybody except Mama. Faith and Ruth were both silent in their own bedrooms, each still trying to wrap their mind around what they just witnessed. David had a night shift at the movie theater, and would later have to come home to the lifeless atmosphere of the Singleton household. Poor James just lay upon his bed, crying in his bedroom until he fell asleep.

Evelyn spent the rest of the night singing praises to her Lord as loudly and passionately as she could.

Are you uncomfortable yet?...

Chapter 3
Something Terrible

    A couple of weeks had gone by and things were starting to go back to normal in the Singleton household. Everybody seemed to get past James's birthday disappointment and went back to living their normal lives.

    James was able to get past his let down because David was a great big brother. A couple of days after the incident, David showed up in his room with a giant bag. The eldest Singleton had used up his entire paycheck to purchase all of the movies that James had wanted for his birthday. Of course, David told his brother to keep it a secret from Evelyn because they didn't want her to get any crazy ideas.

    A few days later than that, David worked a Sunday morning shift at the movie theatre. He was in charge of the box office outside, which sold movie tickets and provided customer service. The job itself was very bittersweet; it had its pros and cons.

    He loved how slow it always was in the early mornings compared to how busy it was on a Friday night. For his morning shifts, David would typically bring a book from home and read throughout the duration. Waves of guests came every ten to twenty minutes, and David would quickly sell them tickets and see them off to the inside of the theater.

Afterward, when all was quiet and he was again alone, he was free to settle back into his book.

It was so mellow in the box office that David saw it as an escape from his crazy religious mother. He loved the people that he worked with, as well. Home was a mix of crazy, shy, and introverted people who only had each other. He needed to get away and retreat to the real world.

David never told anyone what his life was like behind closed doors. Likewise, he did not share much of what he did outside of the home with his mother or siblings. They were two worlds that could not cross. He did not want it to get back to his mother what he really thought about her and her religion.

So, he played the waiting game. At 17 years of age, he was already applying for different colleges that would allow him to live on campus, and he only had a couple of months left in the school year. He was almost rid of his crazy life at home.

Another benefit of his job was how easy it was. How hard was it to hear the name of a movie someone wanted to see, then select it on a screen? He loved selling things; it was practically a game to him. A customer would walk in and David would mention a special VIP card he had to sell. Often, they would say no to the offer. David always had a stroke of genius and brought them back. "Are you sure you don't want this Sir? It is only five dollars and you would never miss out on pre-screenings."

"Pre-screenings? As in, I can see this film before it comes out?"

"Yes! That is exactly what I mean! How could you miss out on that free pre-screening? Play movie critic and write the review on it too."

"Oh, why not! I will take the VIP card!"

David loved every minute of it, he felt he could do great as a car salesman. But that was not his goal, his goal was to get away from home.

His job inside of the box office only had one con, and that was the elderly. He absolutely hated dealing with them. The younger guests knew what they wanted to see, and they already knew the time of their movie showing. They were quick and simple.

Elderly folks were a different story. It never failed, David would be sitting in the box office, enjoying his book until he glanced up and out of the glass separating him from the outside world. He would see something like an old lady parking in the very back of the parking lot when there were a bunch of spots open in the front. That was the first thing that irritated him. Then he watched her from a distance slowly making her way towards him. The old woman would drag her little walker on the ground and slowly continue to inch her way towards the box office. All of the frustration filled up his imagination. His stress-free day was about to get miserable.

What was going to be the issue that day? Was she going to take ten whole minutes looking through her purse to find her money? 'Oh, I am sorry dear, I should have come prepared. I cannot find my pocketbook that has my money in it.' Is she going to inch her way to the front and decide then and there what movie she wants to see? 'What do you have playing today?' 'Well Ma'am, look up at the screen, we have all the titles.' 'Ohhhhhhhh… Hmmmmmm… Ohhhhhh. What is Star Wars?' This old lady should have had this figured out before she got here!

By then the line would be building up, and people would be starting to get impatient. Was she going to complain about random things that were irrelevant to her even seeing a movie? 'You guys oughta clean the glass a little bit better. All I can see are tiny fingerprints all over the glass! I am about to complain to the manager about this!'

It was like, Lady, seriously… You have to look at this glass for one second to see me and buy your ticket.

Maybe she will take forever to pick a movie, pick it, then show up a few minutes later for a refund. This means a lengthy process on the computer, all while the line was building up.

He recalls a time where an old lady showed up and said, "I would like one to the 3D movie."

"Okay, well we have a lot of 3D movies. Can you please let me know which one?" David replied.

"You know... the 3D movie!" the old woman insisted.

"Ma'am, there is a 3D version of all the movies we are playing. I need the name." By this time, David was gritting his teeth.

"I don't know the name! I just want the 3D movie!"

"So you want to see Zootopia?" David chose a random movie from the screen, the one with the nearest showtime.

"Yes, the 3D movie," the woman said, momentarily pacified.

David sold her the ticket for Zootopia in 3D, and then happily sent her on her way. But, twenty minutes later she returned, furious. "I said I want one to the 3D movie!"

"Ma'am, this movie is 3D," David pointed out, affecting his best calm.

"No! It is not the right movie! I just want the 3D movie!"

It was just too much for David. He got a job so he could leave the craziness, not dive into it.

Some of the elderly folks were very funny though. The old-timers who were stuck in their prime generation would crack him up. David remembered once an old man walked up to the box office, set his cane aside, and let his mind and mouth run free.

"Son, I would like one ticket to Hacksaw Ridge. Let me tell ya! I have been to war before and these movies do not do it justice, so I hope this one will. I done killed about fifty Japs in my day, and there was never a camera that turned away! You see the whole nine! Look at all these lazy children in lines with their cell phones. They need to be drafted, every one of them! Make them work! Make them do something! I am retired, I earned this movie!" The old man would go on and on.

"Yes sir, you did, here is your ticket. Enjoy."

Life in the box was crazy. Many different types of people would show up, talk to you, and give you their life stories.

He felt like his days were numbered at his job. Before he knew it, an acceptance letter could show up in the mail and take him away from everything. He would miss the job though.

David was wrapping up his shift that Sunday when he got a phone call from one of his best friends, Jason.

He answered the phone out of sight and put it on speaker. "Hey man, let me call you back. I am wrapping up work, and I have some people walking up to the glass."

"Thaaaa boyyyyyy! Hurry up and call me back! Let's hang out!"
"Sure thing." Click.
Jason was one of a few close friends that David had. He had long black hair and wore glasses. He went through different wardrobe phases every few months. Last year he was all about hoodies. A few months later, he wore nothing but band t-shirts and skinny jeans. His next phase was regular sized jeans and polo shirts. Currently, he was in a black t-shirt phase. He had the most interesting personality of all his close friends, mainly because there were so many layers to his character. He was funnier than his other friends. He could seriously succeed as a stand-up comedian if he wanted to, and David told him this all the time. The way he would switch up his voice from high to low a thousand times throughout a conversation was very entertaining. His facial expressions and body movements matched his comical personality perfectly. The timing of his jokes was unmatched, and this made it fun to hang out with him.
Unlike everyone else, Jason was aware of everything that went on at the Singleton household.
Jason was a very deep thinker for someone so funny. For example, when he saw the grass, he did not just see the grass. He saw the beauty of it, the detail, the very things that made it breathtaking, and

what made each thing significant in its own right. It was never just grass, sky, ocean, or space. He saw complicated things in seemingly simple things. He could see thousands of beautiful colors in what appeared to be a single colored portrait. This is what made Jason one of David's favorite people to talk to when anything was on his mind. He just had such a unique perspective on everything.

He was also very supportive of anything David wanted to do. Jason was the only person who would genuinely ask about the different schools he applied to, or ask about his mother's crazy moments, or even if anything interesting was on his mind lately. At times Jason seemed more enthusiastic about David's dreams than David was. It felt good to be supported, to have somebody who believed in him.

But there was also a darker side to him, though. He battled with deep depression. Without reason, even in the happy periods of his life, a dark feeling could hit out of nowhere. Jason described it as gravity bearing down on him a thousand times heavier than air, like life was sucked out of everything bright and beautiful. Even in a room full of family and friends, David confessed that he felt alone. And nothing could take the feeling away.

Sometimes the depression would be too much to deal with alone, and he would call up David and express an interest in ending his life. He could not endure the domino effect of his emotions as he spiraled further down into utter despair. A singular negative feeling about anything descended into negative thoughts, and those negative thoughts led to even more until Jason felt buried, suffocated. No matter how obvious it was that these thoughts were lies, manipulations of reality, they always seemed convincing at the moment.

    David related to Jason's depression. Sometimes David felt guilty about finding relief in his best friend's suicidal thoughts, too, because he felt them strongly himself. Life was hard, it does not yield to you. It does not compromise or care about you. That was why David lived where he lives. That was why his father left him when he and all his siblings needed him the most.

    Fear often consumed David from the inside out. What if he never got out? What if he shot for the stars and never succeeded? His brother and sisters looked up to him for a faith he didn't even possess. What kind of disappointment would they feel if they knew their big brother was a false hero? Who wants to wait for the moment of their reckoning? The only answer to this pain was to end it. The only way out was to die. Sometimes this was what made the most sense to David. Ultimately, in that part of his brain that always felt reasonable, he knew this was not the answer, but sometimes he just felt too much. But With Jason, he was not alone, and that is why he felt relief in the midst of Jason's depression.

David and Jason both lived in the same neighborhood, so all he had to do was drop his car off at home and walk a few blocks over. When he reached Jason's house, he was greeted with the warmest welcome from his parents. It always felt great to be this appreciated. It never failed, every single time he walked into this house, Jason's parents nearly threw a party for him. If only his house was like this. Why couldn't he just be a part of a normal family?

Jason's mom looked at him gratefully and said, "Jason is in his room upstairs, feel free to walk right in."

"Thank you," he replied casually but sincerely. He grabbed onto the railing of the stairs as he quickly made his way up to Jason's bedroom.

Whenever he walked into Jason's bedroom, he was always immediately taken away by it. This was seriously the coolest bedroom ever, especially when it was compared to David's meager own. The one giant window in the room was covered by a black sheet with a white solar system design. The walls were all painted black and each had designs of their own. In the middle of the ceiling was the fan, and the black light that was screwed into the fan was what brought the room to life. The bulb would cast a strange glow in the dark and make it look like you were surrounded by all kinds of strange, surreal things. David knew he would never be allowed to get away with a trippy room like this at his own house.

His friend was lying on his bed reading a book when he noticed the door open. "Dude! What's up! Come on in!"

Jason was always so enthusiastic when David stepped into his presence, his love matching the love of his parents.

David began to feel the excitement and yelled, "It's the boyyyyyy!"

Jason grinned and in a cheerful manner, "It's the boyyyyyy!"

Closing the bedroom door behind him, David looked at his friend and noticed the book he was reading. A perfect start to a conversation would be to ask what it was about.

"I didn't know you could read," David said sarcastically.

Jason laughed and replied, "Oh yeah, I can read two whole sentences in this bad boy! But no, all jokes aside, this book is groundbreaking!"

"Well, what's the book about?" David loved to read, and always looked for recommendations on what to read next.

A pure look of excitement took over Jason's entire countenance, from his eyes all the way into how he positioned his body on the bed. He always got excited when he had a new thought to share. He could go on for hours about it, and David never got bored of listening.

Jason composed himself as he sat up and said, "It is about the law of attraction."

"The law of attraction?" David had never heard anything about that outside of science class.

"Yes! It is the belief that positive thoughts will bring positive things, and negative thoughts will bring negative things."

David paused, considering, before he finally said, "Well, no duh. This is common sense. Why do you need a book to tell you this?"

Excitement all but oozed out of Jason's pores, undeterred by David's cynicism, and his hand motions became even more flourished as he continued to speak on about the revelatory greatness of what he had been reading.

"The boy just doesn't get it! Do you not understand the power of your mind? All of our failures begin with a thought. A doubt. The very moment where our mind starts to tell us something is impossible. It leads to being too afraid to conquer something big, which can lead us to failure. Well, every success story started with a thought, a positive thought at that!"

Jason's enthusiasm was infectious, and David was gradually beginning to understand the point his friend fought eagerly to make. As usual, David was beginning to see common sense, in awe that his best friend was seeing so much more.

After a soft breath David said, "Yeah, I guess you're right man."

Jason leaped off of his bed, a look of intensity beginning to mix with his comedic enthusiasm, launching into an impassioned speech, "Can you imagine what life would be like if every great idea was dismissed? What if Stephen King kept the idea for Carrie crumbled up in the trash can? What if the artist who created your favorite album just said, 'Oh, cool idea,' then went on with his day? Do you understand how many amazing ideas we have on a daily basis? But they are just ideas! We don't believe in them enough to turn them into something. You have to give it to the ones who believed in their idea enough to turn it into something great. That is the law of attraction! Someone believed in their idea, had the courage to speak it, and then it happened when they chased after it!"

It really was a cool thought to take in. Maybe this was something David needed to hold onto when it came to getting out of his house. Maybe the law of attraction could play a major role in him getting into a good school. If he believed in it, had the courage to speak it, was crazy enough to chase after it, then it was bound to happen.

His best friend had an amazing knack at opening his mind up, putting David into a place of deep thought. Everything in David's experience had already taught him that nothing was for nothing. There had to be a reason why James would read this book of all books.

Contemplative, David asked his best friend, "So why this book? What's really going on?"

The other boy gazed over for a long pause, his expression and posture becoming more serious. After a deep breath, he said, "I just need something to hold onto buddy. I have brought so much negativity into my world, and I don't feel like I am where I want to be in life."

"Dude, you are 17 years old, you have all the time in the world!" David wasn't trying to dismiss his friend's feelings, but he wanted to give him some perspective if only to comfort him.

But Jason only looked back on him with sadness and said, "True, but I just don't have a vision. I don't know what I am going to do when school is over. I believe I can achieve anything if I put my all into it. I just need something to chase. It seems to make a lot of sense. If I believe in something, I can have it. I just want some hope if I'm being honest."

Everything Jason said David could relate to. Hope was so hard to come by in the Singleton household. Hope was only found in Jesus Christ, God in human form, descended from Heaven to give all an example to live by. Being of flesh, Christ was able to live as a human, and because of this, he was an example to humanity. Accordingly, he lived perfectly, was persecuted, nailed to a cross, and rose again on the third day. In the Singleton household, hope was found in the redemption given to them by Christ, and in the forgiveness of sins granted by his sacrifice.

But how could David hope in something that he couldn't see? How could he trust in something that left him with a crazy mother and without a father? Why did everything that mattered seem to be on his shoulders to bear? It was on him to put in the work and time for school. It was on him to remain good and positive. It was on him to make something of himself. Heck, it was on him to never choose the flesh over his Lord. Where was the help? Where was the supernatural power of Christ at work in his life? If it was always on him, then the law of attraction was truth in his eyes. If David was to believe in anything, he wanted to believe in himself and his potential.

The boys spent the next few hours talking about all kinds of things. The law of attraction, aliens, God, science, depression, the people who were blind to the world, the media, movies, music, everything. It was starting to get closer to nine o'clock at night, and this meant it was time to go back home. David said his goodbyes and started to walk back to his house.

When he got back to his house, it seemed nothing was out of the ordinary. That it was quiet and calm was a big relief to him. Most of all, David was grateful that Mama was not waiting for him by the door. Honestly, he was not in the mood to talk to his mother about anything. He just wanted to keep himself in his room until he had to go to school the next day.

It was dark in the hallway, but David could see that the doors of the rooms looked old and beat up, worn, and the bathroom door was open as usual. The small singular window in the bathroom reflected the moonlight into the hallway, which gave it a creepy glow. Similar to a hotel, all of the rooms were lined in a straight path, one after another. James's room was closest to the front of the hallway, then Ruth's, then Faith's, and then his own. Evelyn's was at the very end. From the front of the hallway, you could see Evelyn's stark red door straight ahead in the middle. The entire door was covered in wooden crosses and pieces of taped on notebook paper. These features were not there before. He quietly worked his way up to her door and to read some of the papers. They were all Bible verses. All of it, including his mother, had made him very uneasy lately. And this unease grew by the day as her patterns became stranger, her faith more ardent.

Ever since she stopped taking her medication, she seemed to cry a lot more. Nobody knew why she was crying. In fact, she didn't even know her kids could hear her, and they never asked her about it the next day. But the Singleton children always heard her in her room weeping and moaning in the night, her wails punctuated now and again by quick mumblings of words that were too quiet and muffled by the walls to make out.

As David was turned away from his mother's door to go into his own room, he heard her faint voice inside. Her voice had a whimpering stutter to it, bursting with sobs, and it sounded agonizing.

"Please Lord forgive me... I-I-I ca-ca-ca-can't imagine how you must feel right now. Ha-ha-ha- how you are looking at your weak servant with sadness and disappointment. I-I-I feel so wicked. I wi-wi-wi-wish these thoughts were not mine. All I want to be is perfect for you Jesus. I-I-I have failed as a mother, I failed as a daughter, I am dirt. Why ca-ca-ca-can't I just be yours? Y-you want devotion. I know that I don't read enough. I know we only talked for two hours today, I-I should never be too busy for you Father. I-I-I de-de-de-deserve to be punished."

It also sounded like she was banging her head on the wall and breaking glass. David did not have it in him to go in and check on her. It reminded him just why he needed to leave this house for good--there was too much darkness. For his own sake, he quit listening in and silently walked into his room.

He got into his bed, laid down, and stared at the ceiling. He could not wrap his mind around the guilt that his mother was expressing. She loved this God with all of her heart; she loved him because he supposedly loved her more. But to David, this did not sound like love.

No, it sounded like fear, obligation, obedience, guilt, shame, anything but love. Why would a being of Love want you to sound like that? If God was real, was this pleasing to him? Did he want his servants to be this broken? To carry this burden on themselves with every breathing moment?

It just seemed unhealthy. This was not proving to be mentally healthy for his mother.

But who cares? David thought in a flash of hostility and anger. She chased his father away, and soon he would be gone himself.

He woke up Monday morning ready to go to school. As his siblings ate breakfast, he made it a point to not interact too much with his mother. He said hello to his family, grabbed some Pop-Tarts, and quickly left the house. He walked to the bus stop and waited for it to arrive. When he finally got on the bus, he worked his way to the back where Jason and his two other close friends always sat, glad to be out of his gloomy house and into their brighter presence.

Of his friends, there was Travis, who resembled a punk rock kid. He was a skinny boy with long black hair that draped over the left eye, and who wore skinny jeans and Vans. Everyone told him that he looked similar to Tom Delonge from the band Blink-182. He was the first friend that David had made when he transferred to his high school. One day there was an assembly and Travis overheard him talking about the movie *A Nightmare On Elm Street*. David happily chimed in because he knew a lot about the movie. David had to watch a lot of movies and listen to most music behind his mother's back. His taste in entertainment was not something she would ever approve of, which was surprisingly the same for Travis, so they also bonded over having strict parents.

Travis' knowledge of movies and music was impressive. He knew everything about Slipknot, Korn, Marilyn Manson, Blink-182, My Chemical

Romance, etc. Nobody at school seemed to appreciate the movies and music that David was into, so it was great to find someone who did. They hit it off after a week. Because the next day after they met, during lunch, David blew Travis off. He chose to sit with his popular group of friends instead. He thought about it after, felt bad, and started sitting with Travis at his table. They hung out every day ever since.

    Then there was Michael. He was the carefree one of the bunch. He grew up a church kid and had a close relationship with Jesus. But he was really fun to hang around. This kid had no filter, so he had a tendency to make the other kids defensive and uptight. He didn't curse or act in any way that would contradict his faith, but he still had no filter and would say whatever was on his mind. He had to do it. If someone was fat, he would unintentionally and very innocently tell them they were fat. It was funny! The other boys would give that look of awe while he just went on with his day. The most popular band at school called "Dragon Slayer" was even upset with him. They spoke passionately about their name and where it came from, but all Michael had to say about it was that it sounded like a video game. The band members got so worked up about it and he just couldn't understand why.

    He was also the student in biology class who would casually rip evolution. The teacher would get very worked up and throw all kinds of facts at him about the theory, but Michael would simply reply, "Dude, why don't we have any monkeys turning into people today?" But still, he was as genuine and carefree as could be.

So it was David, Jason, Travis, and Michael. If there was anything David would miss when he left for college, it was his friends. The ones who kept him sane.

When they arrived at school, the four of them stepped off of the bus and into the crowded hallways of their high school. It was always hard to make your way around in the morning because everybody was scattered around the hallways, blocking lockers and doors.

Of the friends, Jason never liked to be in the middle of a large crowd, he never felt like he fit in with the world. It was not hard to tell when he was uncomfortable. He was not afraid of anyone, he just did not like the feeling of being out of place.

Michael spotted a girl in the hallway who was short, but not short enough to be a dwarf. "Is she a little person? Or is she a really short person who is literally on the edge of being a little person?" He said this as if this were a genuine question.

Travis punched him on the shoulder and quietly said, "Bro, shut up. I think that poor girl heard you."

Michael looked very confused like he had no idea what he said or did that was out of line.

Travis immediately turned his attention to David and started quoting some lines from *The Waterboy* to de-escalate the tension. "Captain Insano shows no mercy," he said, trying to mimic Adam Sandler's voice from the movie.

David started laughing and quoted a line back to him, "He spit in the da cooler."

The dialogue between the two of them was like a second language that only they shared. If people had not seen the movies the friends referenced, they would be completely lost in a conversation. The majority of a normal conversation between the two would be full of random movie quotes.

They all spent a few more minutes hanging out together before it was time to head to class. David was about to go to his math class with Ms. Kellbrook. She was his favorite teacher. He had never had a teacher who cared more about him as a student as they did the job itself. She never minded staying after school to help him with homework from any subject, she was very supportive of his dreams to attend a good college, and she was honest with him when she needed to be. She suspected that he went through things at home because from time to time she would ask if he was okay. He always told her that everything was fine, but she was smart enough to know he was struggling with something.

David sat down at his desk and immediately began to nod in and out, drowsy from his lack of sleep the night before.

"David, did you not get much sleep last night?" Ms. Kellbrook asked quietly enough so that none of the other kids could hear.

He smiled up at her and replied, "I actually got a lot of sleep. I just didn't want to wake up this morning."

She smiled back at him agreeably and nodded. "Yes, we all have those days. Anyway, don't you dare fall asleep in my class! You know I will not hesitate to throw a marker at you, drop a textbook on your desk, or make you stand up for the whole period!"

They both started laughing because all three of those things had happened to him for sleeping.

The class went on for the next hour and a half, and it was entertaining. One of the kids actually did fall asleep, and Ms. Kellbrook scared him by dropping a heavy textbook on his desk. The entire class laughed at the way he jolted awake, almost jumping entirely out of his seat.

Math was a complicated and sometimes boring subject by nature, but it never was difficult for David when Ms. Kellbrook was teaching. She truly had a gift for teaching. She broke things down in a way everybody could understand no matter how skilled they were at the subject. In David's experience, most other teachers lacked the patience, passion, and skill that she had as a teacher.

The day went on as any other school day did. It dragged on for what felt like a thousand hours, and lunch with his best friends was the highlight of his day. By the time they were back on the bus, going home, David was unable to pay attention to anything his friends said. He was just nodding yes and giving short answers because he was already thinking about what it would be like when he got home. It felt like his life at home was getting weirder and weirder. He never liked it, but now he was beginning to hate it.

Deep down he was afraid of it getting worse at home, and that eventually, he would have to step in and involve himself. He didn't know how long he could fake it. How long would it be before everybody finally caught onto the fact he was not a Christian? What if his mother continued down this path of wrongdoing and he felt a sense of responsibility to speak up? He just didn't want to deal with anything that would make his life harder than it already was.

Before David knew it, the bus stopped at his street, and he debarked knowing that he would have to deal with life at home now. He walked around the neighborhood, taking his time, working his way up to his house until he found himself standing in front of it. He looked at the parking spot where his mother's car was normally parked and saw her car parked in it.

He took a deep sigh because he was hoping she wouldn't be home. There was no way to know what the rest of his day would bring, but sometimes he would just instinctively know. It was a gut feeling. Dread. A sense that something really bad was going to happen.

A feeling of nausea settled in the pit of his stomach as he turned the doorknob.

"Something terrible is going to happen today," he silently predicted.

Chapter 4
Innocence

"I am a freak."

That was the inner dialogue of James Singleton as he sat in the back of the classroom. Everyone looked so happy, so preoccupied with the people around them. Everybody was smiling, laughing, vying for each other's attention. A boy and girl could be seen staring at each other like they were the only ones in the room. A group of friends could be heard enthusiastically hyping up a new video game. Even the less popular kids had a group of their own. They were okay with being the school's rejects because they still had a group to belong to.

But he was the freak that nobody paid attention to. He had learned how to live inside his head because there was nothing much for him outside of that. Nobody ever made fun of him, but he may as well not exist.

James sometimes wondered if the other kids were afraid of him. If he was completely honest with himself, maybe they should be. They wouldn't be able to spend a single moment inside of his head, he knew that for sure. He didn't always have the purest thoughts, and sometimes he scared himself.

Ultimately, he had no one to talk to, and even if he did, nobody would truly understand him. Truth was, he could hardly understand himself. He used to wonder if it was normal for him to not have friends. Now he was almost certain, to the outside world, he was something inherently abnormal, and all of the other kids could sense it.

***

As David stepped into the house, he felt a sense of unease. Or maybe this was one of those moments when anxiety got the best of him. The sensation caused him to feel a tight tug in the pit of his stomach, nurtured by the fear of the unknown. His mind worked against him, playing on a loop of various scenarios that would most likely never happen.

What would it be? Would he enter into a home of dead bodies?

Never.

Maybe he would find every possession of his was given to the less fortunate.

Never.

His mom stopped acting crazy and no longer believes in the Bible.

Definitely never.

The house was quiet that day. The only thing David heard was the TV in the living room. As he made his way there, he found Evelyn on the couch staring lifelessly into the screen. She was very stiff yet zombie-like in her gaze as if she were watching the TV but not focused on it. Playing wasn't even a television station she would enjoy. Evelyn watched golf. She looked like she had just woken up, her hair was messy, and her pajamas were stained.

He was feeling increasingly creeped out by Evelyn's demeanor, and he even forgot he was standing in the doorway absolutely frozen and staring at her. But she didn't seem to notice or care about the look on his face. He felt like he needed a conversation starter, he was beginning to look rude.

"Hey Mom," he said, as politely as he possibly could. She just kept staring blankly into the television screen. No movement, it was hard to even tell she was breathing. "No work today Mom? I hope you're not sick, feeling okay?"

But she kept staring into the screen, not a peep, not a breath, not a single expression on her face. Fear began to take over his body. He found his hands shaking and his heart beating twice as fast. The moment was unpredictable. She really lost her mind, this was beginning to look all too familiar to him.

David's mind went back a decade to when he was seven years old, finding his mother in this exact lifeless position. His father was at work at the time, and it was a rainy Saturday morning.

"Mama, what are you watching?" the child had asked. But there still came no response. With a confused look on his young face, he asked another innocent question. "Mama? Are you okay?"

The silence in the room made the rain pattering outside seem too loud, and fear was starting to settle in. But his mother just kept staring lifelessly into the screen, oblivious to his presence and voice.

Slowly and gently he approached his mother and put his hand on her shoulder, hoping to rouse something in her. Before he could even say her name, she suddenly screamed and grabbed him by the wrist. Her thin, bony hand squeezed harder until it felt like a shark was applying pressure to take a bite out of its prey.

Young David began to cry hysterically and scream in pain. "Let go, Mama! Please!" But she kept screaming and was now jerking his little wrist with great force.

She rose from her seat and started to drag his body violently around the living room floor. He kept screaming, he kept crying. He felt the agonizing burn from the carpet as his skin dragged against it. He kept crying out, "I'm sorry! I'm sorry, Mama! Please! Just stop!"

But she wouldn't stop. Instead, she placed her knee on his back and grabbed a handful of his hair, pulling it hard and tight. As David screamed louder, she began to rain down blows to the back of the head. After a while, David's mind and soul seemed to leave his body. Everything was numb, fuzzy, and he did not feel the pain anymore. He stopped screaming, but she kept beating him in flurries of slaps and punches.

"You will never hurt me again! I won't ever let you take the best of me again!" she yelled as she beat David. He realized that instead of him, his mother saw someone else. She wasn't even in the present moment, she was in her past, imaging he was someone else.

Why was she like this? It was difficult to ask this question in the heat of the moment. It's not as if she would have heard him anyway. But it was a question that crossed his dazed mind. It was obvious that his mother suffered from some kind of sickness, but David was too young to understand what kind. She was so angry all the time. Where did this come from? He found it hard to believe that people were just hateful by nature, so something must have happened to her in the past to make her that way.

The Singleton children didn't know too much about anyone else in their family. Everybody was distant and David often wondered if that was for a reason. Why did they never spend time with their Grandma and Grandpa? Did they have something to do with the way his mother was? Maybe she came from a house of abuse, and it had made her bitter. When someone comes from a house of severe control, they usually become someone who has to maintain complete control.

Mama controlled everything: what they believed, what they did, what they wore, and who they were friends with. She wore 'the pants in the family' even when his father was around. The Singleton patriarch could make all the money in the world and pay every bill in the house, but Mama still maintained complete control.

Were her parents ashamed of her? Is that why they never tried to call or make an effort to be a part of their lives? It was possible.

It must have been something terrible that she had to live through because the beatings were too intense. He was being beaten like he was someone else in her life who deserved it. It felt like she was releasing something pent up, and he was nothing more than a tool that cleansed her of her secret burdens.

All he ever wanted was to feel safe in his mother's arms. But how could he ever feel safe? It was impossible, and each bruise that bloomed to life on his body destroyed more and more of his innocence.

He could even recall a moment where he actually prayed to Jesus. As his mother beat him ruthlessly, he prayed for God to save him. But, of course, God never came to his aid. No, he just sat on his heavenly throne and watched the violence happen. Even at a young age, David caught onto the harsh truth that God would never save him. Nobody could, and all he felt at this moment was hopelessness.

God felt like the biological father who was never interested in being a father. The one who never shows up to be a part of his child's life. God was the father who dropped his child off at foster homes. David felt like the son who always called and had no response, like the son who waited every day for his father to pick him up only to be let down. *How could my father leave me here like this?* That was always the perpetual question that remained always in the back of his mind.

Finally, David snapped out of it and found himself back in the moment. Evelyn was now staring at him with a peaceful smile.

"How was school today honey?" she said politely as if none of what happened actually did.

In return, David tried to quickly compose himself and bury the awkwardness he felt.

"It was okay Mom. School is school," he said, wincing in pain as he moved, certain he would be feeling this for a while. Still, he wondered why she wasn't at work today, and now that he had her attention, he was able to ask her about it. "Mom, why did you stay home today?"

She looked back at him with proud confidence and said, "I was let go for sharing my faith." It was obvious that she felt very accomplished about this.

David's mind was now running all over the place with new questions. He looked back at her with concern and asked her to explain further: "I don't understand."

"I was making the most of every opportunity I had, honey. I was sharing the news of God's great love a little too much for my coworkers. My boss said I was making people uncomfortable." She had a look of genuine disbelief on her face as she told her story, looking as if she could not comprehend why they had rejected her when what she was giving them was a genuine gift.

What did this mean? This meant that he would have to deal with his crazy mother even more now. It meant the bills may not get paid, and they would be put out on the street when eviction happened due to nonpayment. Worst of all? It was more time for her to lose her mind and terrorize him and his siblings.

She was crazy! How could she do this to them as if none of their wellbeing mattered to her?

No conversation they could have would go anywhere. Her belief was too deep. What consoled David was the knowledge that he would be leaving for college soon.

So, he just put on a fake smile and told her what she would want to hear. "It's like what we read before, Mom. Paul was put in chains for the Gospel. You planted the seeds and it is up to the Holy Spirit to water them." He could barely believe the words coming out of his mouth. He felt his body cringe as he spoke what felt like another language. Speakings things that he did not believe.

To no surprise, his mother lit up and embraced him. "We are going to be alright," she said with infallible confidence. But all David felt was apprehension.

Before he could respond, the door opened and his siblings were home from school.

Ruth was the first to run full force towards Mama. She happily jumped into her mother's arms and hugged her tight.

"How was school today, sweetheart?" Mama asked.

"It was okay I guess. My teacher got irritated because I wouldn't let her teach false information," said Ruth enthusiastically. Sometimes she seemed so much like Mama in her beliefs that it chilled David to the core.

"She wanted us all to give a take on being equal," Ruth explained. "and I was trying to tell everyone that as believers, we are set apart. We don't look like the world. We look like Jesus. She kept going back and forth with me about how other students who may believe differently are also unique. I asked her why my opinion was not being honored as equal. She gave up on the conversation, so I guess I won." Ruth was on Mama's lap swinging her feet back and forth with a big smile on her face, her composure excited. Mama looked back at her with a proud look and spoke of how thankful she was to have Ruth as her daughter.

Faith took her time walking into the living room and greeted everybody softly, just as quietly describing her day. Her day at school was no different than any other day. She listened in class, passed every assignment with flying colors, and spent lunchtime reading one of the books she got for her thirteenth birthday.

Mama's praise shifted to Faith, and she went on about how Faith was such a good daughter before dismissing both Faith and Ruth to their bedrooms. James didn't have much to say about his day, which was not unusual.

"So, James, tell me about your day," said Mama.

He seemed confused, a bit awkward, but told her his day was fine.

"Not much to say about it, honey?" his mother pressed.

David casually chimed in and spoke for his brother, "School is school Mom."

She looked at David with an expression of irritation, but she still cracked a smile. "Okay James, you can go too."

James did not hesitate to head to his room, glad to be done with the conversation. As David started to make his way out of the living room, though, Evelyn called his name.

He turned back around and she said, "Your brother can speak for himself."

All David could say back was, "Yeah, sorry, I was just..." but she interrupted him.

"It's okay, it's okay. Just go do whatever you were going to do." Her hand waved as if dismissing him.

David quickly made his way down the hallway and into his bedroom.

As he fell into his mattress, David's body went limp and he sunk into his soft mattress. He still ached from the beating his mother had given him. But he tried to relax and stare off into space, eyes pointed to the empty ceiling. His mind began to think on its own again.

All of a sudden, he was seven years old again at the dinner table with his Mom, Dad, and younger siblings. His body was hurt from the previous day's beating. A beating so severe that he was still petrified to be in his mother's presence. How could she just sit there and act so peaceful? Like she didn't remember screaming like a maniac and beating her eldest son.

Their conversation at the table was very casual. How was work? Dad informed his family that he got a raise for his good effort. But, his boss still rode his back. The conversation was focused on work until Dad looked at David with a puzzled expression.

"What happened to David?" Dad had not missed David's bruises or the languid, disconnected way he moved.

Mama very casually told him that David fell while he was at work.

Dad looked at his son almost in disbelief. "Well, are you okay? How did it happen?"

David didn't know what to say, but before he could say anything, Mama interrupted. "We don't need to get into all that and remind him! Just eat!"

His dad quickly got himself together and reached out for the steak sauce.

As he started to pour the sauce on his plate, Mama's face twisted with irritation. She reached over and snatched the sauce from Dad's hand and launched into a screaming tirade. As her shrill, loud voice filled the air, steak sauce flung from the bottle that she jerked and waved and hit David in the face.

But Mama did not notice as she ranted at Dad. "I seasoned this! I worked really hard making dinner for *all of you* tonight! What? Is my steak not good enough for you?"

Dad just sat there with a look of pure shock and confusion on his face. "Honey, I love your steak, I just..."

"Shut up!" she yelled, not letting him finish. "You are ruining the taste I wanted this to have. You don't see David trying to change it, do you?"

Dad just took a deep breath and gave in like he always did, seeking to de-escalate more than defend. "Okay, I'm sorry."

Mama's breaths came hard and short, something like pants as she tried to calm herself down. Her eyes shifted and she looked at David and said, "Honey, when a woman takes her time to season a steak, you should never be rude like your stupid father and make it taste differently."

"Yes, Mama," seven-year-old David replied nervously.

As the memory came to an end, David was pulled back to the present, laid still in his bed, looking at the ceiling. Reflecting on his past, he asked himself questions he may never know the answers to. Why did Dad never stand up to her? Why did she always have to be right? Did he know she beat him as a child? Was Dad truly afraid to stand up for his son, all of his children, and get everybody out and away from her? What filled David was hate, hate toward his father as deep and dark as the hate he felt for his mother.

What a coward, David thought venomously. Their dad left all of his children behind with a crazy woman. He left her to be a single parent, responsible for the bills and raising four children. David was thankful his siblings were too young to remember this side of their mother. After Dad left the family, they had a period of peace, calm. She stopped her abuse after Dad left the family. By then, she was on her medication and found God. To his siblings, she was a saint. But David knew better. To him, she was a ticking time bomb just waiting to go off. It was just a matter of time.

Dad missed everything: birthdays, holidays, school functions, graduation, all of it. Worst of all, he chose to do that. How could a man turn his back on his kids? David began to tear up as his mind dug deeper into the thought. Because he had to grow up without his father, he had to learn how to be a man on his own.

Worst of all, he could not help but think his father's absence was a reflection of his own worth.

What was wrong with him to make his own father walk away forever? He felt so much anger inside all the time.

There were moments where David felt okay, but something in him remained wounded by his father's abandonment. As a result, he often made harsh decisions. He had made many friends through the years that he considered close, but as soon as they wronged him in any way, it was easy for him to leave them behind. He never cared to mend his broken friendships and gave walking away no second thought. He also found it hard to trust anyone. He was nice to the friends he did have- he loved them and his family- but he would never completely put himself out there. He did not consciously blame his dad for his coldness because he did not feel like he was the reason he behaved this way. David felt like this was just who he was at his core. It was his nature. But where did it come from?.

If he were to stand face to face with his father, he imagined it would be awkward. While David had never been one to hate people, he would feel hatred towards his father. He wondered why all of his friends had awesome, normal fathers, but he was left with a pathetic and scared little man. A man who could not stand up to his wife or rescue his children.

David realized that his pillow was wet from sweat that dripped from his hair, his face covered in tears. He wept more than he realized. It surprised him because he didn't sit around and cry about his dad too often anymore. But still, he had his hard days, especially when his mother was particularly awful.

He sat up, cleaned off his tears with his shirt, and focused on the sound of his breathing. Since he was already taking the time to self reflect, why not see what else he could figure out about himself?

Aside from his hatred towards his father, what about his mother? Was he afraid of her? Why should he be? He was grown up so she couldn't physically hurt him like she did when he was a little boy. What was she really going to do to him if he decided to speak his mind from this point on? It annoyed David that he was passive like his father when it came to conflict with his mother. He always told himself, why argue?

But maybe that was a cop-out. Maybe the truth was that he *was* afraid of his mother. If he defied or challenged her in any way, would the scared and helpless little boy take over when she retaliated? Deep down he wondered if this was why he carried on lying about his faith. Lying about how he felt.

In many ways, nobody in his family knew who he really was. He felt safe this way. But why does he need to feel safe? He was grown up, by age an adult. So, why was it hard to be himself? He felt it deep inside- a ticking time bomb. It would not surprise him if he blew up one day and told it like it really was.

He heard a knock on his door and in walked Ruth. "Hey, big brother," she said.

David smiled and asked her what she wanted.

"Now, see, I was just wondering if... You... Could maybe...." The girl seemed to hesitate a bit.

"Spit it out, Ruth," said David with a chuckle.

Ruth smiled and began to attack him with hugs and yelled, "Ice cream, ice cream, we all want ice cream!"

David laughed and tried to block his sister's attacks. "Okay, get James and Faith, and we will drive to get some ice cream."

Ruth was freaking out at this point and ran to gather the other siblings before he was even out of bed.

When the siblings announced their plan to their mother, who was cooking dinner, she tried to stop them from having ice cream before eating their meal. But the kids begged and begged her to let their older brother take them out, and she surprisingly relented and gave them permission.

The car ride was very entertaining. David had forgotten how comfortable they all were with each other when they were together as a group. Apart from one another, James and Faith were very quiet, and Ruth was not likable. But together, it was nothing but laughing and giggling. They played riotous games with each other like the cheesy punch buggy game. It was a happy but loud car ride with everyone punching each other, making jokes, and just living in the moment.

They reached the small ice cream parlor where they were going to get their desserts and decided to eat inside. The shop was a small diner with tables outside. Because the weather was beautiful, teenagers hung out in groups all over the place. This was one of the popular hangout spots. For once, the Singleton children were not by themselves looking at all the groups of friends. They were family and had a group of their own. Nobody had to feel like a loser or freak.

David, taking in the wonderful moment, cementing this happy memory, realized something. There was an innocence about his siblings that he wished he had. They were all so happy, so carefree, that it was easy to tell they were unharmed, unscathed by their mother. It didn't seem like they had too many questions or saw the world for the hell-hole it really was. They all had no problems with their faith the way that David had. He watched silently as each took time to pray before they ate their ice cream.

He was happy, though, to have taken the beatings that his siblings would have taken otherwise. It was better him than them in his mind. He was thankful they were either too young to remember, or never witnessed, the things that happened to him. They had an innocence about them that he was happy to see. That's why they came together as a family and laughed with no worries. Of course, David wished he had this innocence because it left a long time ago. The innocence was beaten out of him each time Dad would go to work. Everything his mother felt his father failed at, David was abused for. It was not always physical. Sometimes it was getting screamed at, belittled as a child, afraid to even take a breath because it would probably be considered obstinate. Yes, he lost his innocence when life became second-guessing everything he said or did as a child. But a smile still started to find its place on him because his brother and sisters had that innocence he lost.

"Maybe he would have never left us if you were never born," said Evelyn to a younger David one night when she tucked him in. She had no consistency when it came to her moods. She could be loving towards him one day and hateful to him the next. Tears had filled his eyes as he lay still in his bed, eyelids closed firmly to feign sleep. He hoped that she would think he was asleep and leave his bedside.

"I know you can hear me you little delinquent," grunted Evelyn harshly, unconvinced by his act. She put her hand on his shoulder and squeezed harder and harder as she grew more frustrated.

David often wondered if there was something psychological about how he felt towards his mother. Even as a bigger man, he feared her. He was terrified of her to disagree, and he did his best to avoid confrontation with her. Maybe he hated his mother for making him feel weak, powerless, and small. His friends treated him like the leader he would never be. His friends always looked to him for advice and guidance. But didn't they see how weak he was? How uncertain and afraid? He had the same relationship with his younger siblings. They saw him as strong and confident when, in fact, his mother had taken every bit of confidence from him.

After they finished their ice cream, they returned home with smiles on their faces, still brimming with giggles. David hung his car keys on the board placed on the wall next to the door and picked Ruth up, putting her on his shoulders. As a group, they walked into the living room to ask about dinner. But as soon as they filtered into the room, they balked. Because Evelyn sat there, an angry look darkening her face. The laugher that had filled the siblings died immediately, and silence filled the room.

David slowly placed his sister back on her feet and stared directly at his mother. Instinctively, he began to move in front of his siblings as if to block them.

"I told you no," Evelyn said under her breath.

David, with a confused look, still smiled as if he could appease their mother and said, "No Mom, you said we could go."

The children all looked at Evelyn and watched her shake with anger. "I just don't get it. What sin did I commit to not have the respect of my children?"

Ruth quickly tried to comfort Mama, but the angry matriarch held her hand up and Ruth came to a stop. "Mama, you didn't do anything wrong, no sin was committed," she still spoke, though, teary-eyed.

Faith and James were both quiet, eyes cast down to the ground.

David stepped tentatively toward Evelyn and calmly reminded her, "Mom, you said no, but changed your mind and gave me permission to take them."

"Shut your mouth, David! Don't you dare defy me!" she yelled harshly.

Even he, used to his mother's anger and rages, was taken aback. He looked at her with a puzzled gaze. "Mom..." he said softly.

"Don't 'Mom' me. I have a bunch of disobedient children roaming around. Clearly, I have done something wrong for the Lord to put me through this." She rose and paced the floor back and forth, still shivering in anger.

"Mama, we're sorry," Faith whispered. She paused and finally walked forward, still staring at the ground. "I felt conviction in my heart, Mama, the moment I left the house and got in the car. I knew I was dishonoring your words. But I wanted to go with them, and I chose my desires over what God wanted. You said no about ice cream and it should have ended there."

"Shut up, you forsaken bastard child!" yelled Mama as if she could not stop herself. Evelyn had come to rest but still shook. It looked like she was trying hard to calm herself down but failed.

A look of pure shock and disappointment was written all over Faith's downcast face, while a look of guilt and regret bloomed upon Evelyn's. "Faith, I appreciate your honesty," their mother said in a more gentle tone, "but this is more my wrongdoing than yours. I must have done something wrong to have this wrong done to me." Tears started to fall down Mama's cheeks.

"Listen to yourself, Mom," said David softly.

"Listen to me," Mama whispered sarcastically. She laughed softly to herself, a menacing chuckle under her breath. "Listen to me. Listen to me? Listen to me!" Her voice grew louder and louder, anger back twisting her face. Her eyes grew twice their size, and the tension in the room was palpable. Finally and unexpectedly, though, she turned her back on her children and walked slowly towards the kitchen. "Listen to me. Listen to me, listen to myself," she mumbled to herself, sniffling and wiping at her tears.

When Mama made her way to the stove, she turned it on as high as it could go. Ruth, James, and Faith were all quiet, sharing looks of pure terror with one another.

"What are you doing Mom?" asked David, fear budding in his gut.

The tears still flowed out of their mother's eyes. As they dripped from her flushed cheeks, they hit the stovetop and made a sizzling sound. Mama would not look at them, ignoring his question. Instead, her arm came out and she quickly rolled up her sleeve.

"Mom, stop, whatever you need me to do, I will do it. Just stop whatever you're doing," David pleaded as cautiously as he could.

Evelyn continued to cry, her falling tears still sizzling as she recited Matthew 13:50. "I will throw them into the furnace of fire, in that place, there will be weeping and gnashing of teeth," she said. Everybody was paralyzed with fear and confusion.

David slowly made his way closer to Evelyn, with his hand out to help her. Still sniffling and crying, she looked at her children and said, "This is just a small fraction of God's punishment on the sin in our life."

Then, before anyone could stop her, she pressed her arm as hard as she could onto one of the stove's burners and held it down. She screamed at the top of her lungs as the stove burned through her skin. The room began to reek of burnt flesh, and the sizzling sounds were drowned out by her high pitch screams. Faith, Ruth, and James began to cry out loudly. David sprung forward, quickly trying to grab their mother, but she slipped out of his hands as she had passed out from the pain and collapsed to the floor.

Chapter 5
Evelyn

Evelyn slowly opened her eyes and realized she was awake. Everything was blurry, and it was difficult to make out where she was at first. With each second that passed, things around her began to settle and focus. She realized she was laying in her own bed, wrapped up in her cold white-feathered blanket. The crosses adorning her bedroom walls came into focus next, followed by her giant dresser, the mirror where she did her makeup, and the old red paint on the walls.

The bedroom floor was littered with scraps of notebook paper. Every day, as she read from her Bible, she would write down what she read. These slips of paper would eventually end up on the floor. There was also a scattering of dirty laundry around her floor as well, along with air freshener cans, broken candlesticks, prescription pill bottles, and plastic bags from the grocery store.

The next thing she noticed was the sharp pain in her right arm. As she rolled over onto her back, the blanket rubbed against her skin and she let out a tiny grunt. Pain shot through her body. She quickly pulled her arm above the blanket and noticed the pattern of dark, deep burn marks.

The sight of her charred flesh took her back immediately to the dramatic moment. Once again, she began to cry, but this time it was silent. Quietly, she whispered Lamentations 5:7 to herself. "Our fathers sinned, and are no more; it is we who have borne their iniquities."

Looking at both of her forearms was an interesting though gruesome sight. The right arm had carved into it a nasty burn, while the left one bore a tattoo of her mother's name in elegant cursive.
Scarlett

She sat up in bed with her head still down and cried as she despairingly tugged at her hair. She hated herself. What sin had she committed against her heavenly father to be punished with the disobedience of her children? Who was paying for who? Was it the sins of her father that brought this onto her? Or was it something she did? The deeper she dug into the question, the harder she pulled her hair.

After a long moment of anguish, she slowly slid out of her bed and worked her way onto the floor. It felt like the weight of the world was on her. Gravity felt so heavy. Maybe she would feel lighter if she cried a little bit more.

That's it!

She had too many tears stored up inside, and she hadn't wept enough. But she was still silently sobbing and dragging herself on her bedroom floor. Pausing every few steps, she would grab onto pieces of notebook paper, read them, and hold them close to her chest. But she couldn't find comfort in anything she had written.

She was so confused, her mind was fuzzy, deeply conflicted. She was having a very hard time coming to terms with the sins of her children and furthermore having to forgive them. If they only knew the price of their sins, the all too often overlooked consequences. The children had no idea what sin did to her, to themselves. Eternity was forever, and Heaven was a wonderful place to spend it. But Hell was something terrifying. She wept even harder over the thought of any of her children drowning in a lake of fire.

James was always her quiet boy, but he would spend his days burning in an unquenchable fire where there was no end to his pain, no end to his high pitch screams. He would no longer be that quiet little boy. Sin would come back to make him speak.

Maybe for their sick pleasure, for the sake of her daughters' displeasure, Faith and little sweet Ruth would be ravaged by Demons by day, and thrown into a tiny room of fire by night. A room so tiny it could cause claustrophobia in even one who was never claustrophobic before. The sweet innocence of her daughters would disappear with every bloody claw mark that scared their skin.

But her son David, who she was most proud of, would suffer the most because he was the leader and the leader was always the hardest to break. He would be nailed to an upside-down cross, which every few hours would catch fire. The flames would be dark blue, the hottest possible flames. He would scream until he couldn't scream anymore. When the flames settled, his skin would be carved up with sharp objects. He would be broken.

It would never end either, this would be there forever. It was an eternity of pain and pure torture. The fire would become all too familiar to them. She found herself crumpled in the middle of her bedroom floor sobbing at the horrific image of Hell. As a mother, she could never allow any one of her children to spend a second in this place. Even she feared spending eternity in the lake of fire and sulfur.

This fear had been an ongoing subject of her prayers lately. For many nights, she found herself at the feet of the cross. The fear of Hell was always enough to bring her into a place of humble surrender. She was great with words, but what could she say against the Lord God himself? His was a level of perfection that could not be fathomed. Big enough to create the self-sustaining universe, big enough to be perfect. She was dirty compared to the light. How could she be enough? Jesus died for her sins, yet she could not live right, and neither could her children.

She slowly looked into her lap and found chunks of torn hair. She was surprised at how much of it she pulled out. But she deserved far much more than her hair being pulled out at the root. As she slowly started to pick herself off of the ground, she looked like a contorted zombie.

Working her way to the vanity where she did her makeup, she sat down, feeling exhausted though she had only just woken. As she looked at her reflection in the mirror, she couldn't help but hate what she saw. As she nodded in and out, she finally came to a stop and kept her head down on the lacquered wood. Tears dripped on her legs as she began to silently pray again.

"Lord, I come to you a humble servant," she whispered passionately. "I come to you with a broken and contrite heart. I kneel before your throne, with my head towards the ground, because I understand I am not worthy to look upon your glory. I should have been a better mother. I may not have been the best example. I know that sin is like a plague, a yeast on a loaf of bread. It spreads, and it leads to death. The sins of my parents have infected me, and now my sins are infecting my children. This burn on my arm does not deliver justice. I deserve far worse. I want to serve you, I want to make you happy, but I am unable. I am just too dirty. I am so sorry, Lord, please have pity on your humble servant. I will do better"

"Is he really this angry, Mama?" When Evelyn heard another voice pierce the silence of her bedroom, she quickly turned around.

It was Ruth, standing sadly outside the door. The child looked heartbroken, confused. The look her daughter had was infectious, and Evelyn immediately felt crushed. Slowly, she got up and walked toward her youngest child. There was a moment of silence between them, and they both took long tearful looks at each other. Finally, they embraced. As Ruth held onto Mama as tight as they could, they both continued to cry.

"I should be so much better for you than I am, sweetheart," said Evelyn in her soft, horse tone. All the crying had finally caused her to choke up and lose her voice. She placed both hands on Ruth's cheeks and looked directly into her eyes. "Unfortunately, our Heavenly Father has not given you the best reflection of himself."

Ruth stood still, hurt and puzzled, unsure of what to say back to Mama.

"Mama, you are the best example I have ever seen. This world is wicked. The kids at my school, the teachers, nobody tries to follow God," said Ruth. Mama still had sadness in her eyes, so she continued to speak. "I have seen your love for the Lord push you to do so many wonderful things, Mama. You have fed the homeless, you take the time to teach us about Jesus, you push us to do good in school. Everything amazing about you is rooted in his word," said Ruth passionately.

Evelyn's eyes glistened with tears bold old and new, but she forced herself to smile and tried to keep herself from crying anymore than she had. "Honey, you give me way too much credit. But I appreciate every kind word you said to me. Just be good from now on. Okay?"

Ruth paused and nodded her head in agreement.

"Good," said Mama quietly. "What time is it baby?"

Ruth had a look on her face like she had some bad news to tell. "You slept through the night, so it's Tuesday. Four o'clock, Mama," whispered Ruth.

Evelyn felt shocked, but she acted casual about it, hugging and kissing her daughter before sending her away.

Though still upset about the sins her children committed against her, she was ready to put it behind her. It killed her to see her youngest one look so heartbroken. This was not a moment to wallow in sorrow, but perhaps it was a moment to teach. She could press on and help her children be better for their Lord and Savior. What she needed was reconciliation with each of her children. Wiping the tears out of her eyes, she pulled herself together and took a breath of fresh air. When at last she felt stable, her tears dried, she stepped out of her bedroom.

David's door was the first one that she knocked on, but there came no answer. She knocked again, a little louder, and still no answer. Slowly and quietly, she opened the door to find he was not in his room. She thought to herself, *"maybe he's at work today,"* and smiled because of how hard-working he was.

The next stop was James, and he was in his room. She opened the door and greeted her son. As soon as she stepped in and said hello, he looked back at her with fear and sadness.

"Is it okay for me to sit next to you for a second, honey?" she asked gently.

James was sitting in his bed, reading a comic book. He nodded yes to her, and she sat on the edge of his bed.

"Are you okay, sweetheart?" whispered Mama.

He looked back at her and quietly nodded.

"I just wanted to let you know that I'm fine. I am not angry with you anymore, and I have made a lot of mistakes," said Mama with as much confidence as she could possibly fake. But, James had nothing to say, he just nodded a third time. Evelyn sighed and began to speak more in a level and peaceful voice. "I made a lot of mistakes that may have brought our family up to this point. I pray you can find it in yourself to forgive me someday."

James looked at the cover of his closed comic book and finally spoke, "I forgive you," he said in a voice so faint that it was almost lost.

Even with his absolution, the atmosphere of his bedroom was as awkward as it could get. It felt like the silence screamed volumes into the space between them. She could never understand why her son was always so unresponsive. His name embodied the meaning of wisdom, so he was supposed to be the child who had the most to say. Yet this was not who he was. But she had faith in her Heavenly Father, and she was certain that there was greatness inside of that pretty little head of his.

She hugged her son tight, kissed him on the top of his head, and told him she often wondered what her quiet baby boy had on his mind all the time. He smiled and told her superheroes, which made her chuckle as she left his bedroom.

It was time for her to talk to Faith. As she quietly walked down the hall and made it to Faith's bedroom door, an overwhelming sense of guilt took her over. Her hands were starting to shake, her eyes were beginning to water once again, and she felt short of breath. In a split second, Evelyn confronted herself with a very hard question: Was the day she brought Faith into their lives the day sin was passed onto her children?

As she stood outside of the bedroom door, her mind began to take her back to the moment Faith became a Singleton.

I watched her every day through a window. While my husband John was at work, I would handle what needed to be handled around the house, and still found myself outside of Chelsea's window. Chelsea was a fifteen-year-old girl who had a baby out of wedlock. Every day I watched this beautiful child tug on her mother's curly brown hair. Her mother was a pretty little thing. She looked like she could have been a cheerleader. But it didn't matter, no girl this young should ever take care of a child. I often looked through the window and felt an overwhelming sense of rage inside of me. I dreaded how this child was going to be brought up.

The young mother still hung out with her friends. This was unacceptable because a baby needed a mother's attention. It was a sin to have a child at this age, so it was time for her to grow up. I also noticed that no boy ever came to hold the child. Where was this beautiful baby's father? It broke my heart to go home to David's father and know that this child will never come home to one.

I watched Chelsea for two months and continued to feel sorrow in my heart for the world of sin this poor child was going to be raised into. With a young lust-filled mother, an absent father, and it did not seem like God was a part of this household. I couldn't see any crosses on the wall, her family never left the house together on Sunday mornings, so who knew what life was like beyond the tiny window I viewed hers through.

I would go home and constantly worry myself to death about this child. The feeling never got any easier, it only grew worse. This baby would probably end up raising itself because the mother would party all night. I could see her being one of those moms who always tries to pawn her kid off on someone else. Looking for a babysitter 24/7 just so she can sleep around. But, at least this child would never be alone. Her mother, whoring around the town, was bound to give this child a brother or sister.

I felt like God was telling me all of this for a reason. I wasn't living under Chelsea's roof, but it was a feeling I had. I felt like I could look at her and see into her very being. I knew she was a whore, ended up with a child, probably never even knew who the father was, and would now ruin this child's life.

It was 3 a.m. when I got the call. I could hear God's voice so clearly in my head. He wanted me to save this child. I was going to raise this baby on my own so that she could have a daddy and a brother. John would never understand, of course, I would have to tell him that I found the child. It wouldn't be a lie-- I did find her, I actually found her in a bad situation. After much prayer and meditation, I knew God had set this child aside for me to mother.

John went to work, and I left the house around 7 a.m. The drive to Chelsea's parent's house was an exciting one. I remember feeling nervous, but it was pure elation. I knew in my heart that this child was mine, and she was going to have a loving family.

I parked the car nearby and kept myself at a distance. The plan was to watch the house and wait for my chance to approach. I had grown to learn when all the daily routines took place in their household. I learned when Chelsea normally took a shower, when the family ate breakfast, when the parents went to work, and when Chelsea left the house. My plan was to wait for her to take a shower. I knew the playpen was in the living room, so I would have a clear sight of my child through the front window. All I had to do was save her when Chelsea was in the shower. Eventually, after a few more minutes, both of the parents left first, which left

Chelsea by herself. This meant she would take a shower soon.

I sat in my car across the street and watched through the windows. This must have been predestined for me because all the windows had no blinds to shield my view. They were using the beautiful weather and the light from the sun to bring life to their home today. I watched Chelsea play with my child for a little bit, then she walked out of sight until she popped up in a window upstairs. This meant she was following her regular routine of taking a shower.

It was such a memorable moment for me because my heart beat fast with excitement. This felt very much like the God of the Old Testament. God would bring his chosen people outside the gates of civilization and tell them, "All you see is yours, just trust in me, and take what I have already given you." This felt like the same thing to me because this was my child, whom I watched from outside of the enemy gates, and my Lord was telling me to simply take what He had already given me. I started to walk in faith towards the house. I approached the front door, said a prayer, and very quietly opened the door.

I poked my head inside first to see if I could hear the soft hissing sound of water. I needed to know Chelsea was in the shower. Luckily for me, the shower just started when I opened the door. This *meant that I had time on my side. I walked into the living room with pure tunnel vision; I just wanted my baby. I walked into the living room and saw her lying peacefully in her playpen. I did not want to waste a single moment lingering there gazing at her because I would have a lifetime to look upon her pretty little face. So I reached in and grabbed the child, bringing her to my chest. The shower was still running and I casually walked out of the house. As I made my way to my car, I was amazed at how my baby never cried. She remained calm. She knew who her mommy was.*

When I got home, the baby began crying hysterically. With some patience, I was able to make her fall asleep in my arms. I fell in love instantly. It was only natural to look at her and call her mine. She looked so peaceful, without a single care in this cruel world. Silently, I sang hymns to her in her sleep, and I told her that mommy loved her very much.

When John came home from work, he was surprised when I told him I found this baby in a trash can. I was supposed to be buying groceries, but in my story, I parked the car, said a prayer, and felt the urge to walk around the neighborhood. It took some time, but I convinced him that the baby was ours. I didn't want to call the authorities and risk the baby being raised by the wrong people. I told him it would be amazing to have a daughter. He was not really up for it, but I always have my way with him. By the end of the night, she was ours. We named her Faith.

I spent months bracing for impact, wondering when the knock on the door was going to come. When John saw a news report for a missing child and put two and two together, I waited for the enemy to come and take away the gift that the Lord had set apart for me. But nothing ever happened. Months turned into years, and Faith grew up to love her family. I even told her the truth about her birth parents, that they were young kids who just weren't ready to be parents. I have always felt so much peace about saving Faith from what could have been a tragic life.

But this very moment, in the present time, as I stood outside of her bedroom door, I hoped and prayed that I did not sin against my Lord. Was this the sin that hung over the Singleton household? Even as I doubted, I felt comfort in my heart as another thought popped up. The Lord commanded me to save Faith, and I was obedient. This feeling was not guilt, it was temptation from the Father of Lies. I smiled and...

Opened the door.

Mama saw her daughter doing what she normally did at home after school: reading a book on her bed. When Mama walked in, the girl gave an angelic smile and a soft hello.

"How are you, honey?" asked Mama.

Faith had such a calmness about her that it was hard for Evelyn not to feel calm herself.

The girl smiled gently and said, "I am just fine, but how about you, Mama?"

Evelyn didn't really know what to say to her daughter. *I was not doing all too well. I was upset at all of them for going against what I said. I felt like sin was beginning to have a firm grip on our family, and I just felt I deserved a far worse punishment than I gave myself.*

"I have had better days, sweetheart," said Mama softly, sounding more sorrowful with each word. "I am hurt that you guys disobeyed me and did what you wanted to do. I have been struggling to try to figure out where I went wrong. What did I do to make you all defy me?"

Faith looked like she had something she wanted to say, but her shy personality was not going to let her say it. Evelyn could see it all over Faith's face.

"Do you have anything to say?" asked Mama out of pure curiosity.

Faith paused and looked down at her pillow like she was contemplating if she was going to say anything. After a few quiet moments, Faith composed her face, and when she looked up there was an expression of confidence across it. "I just don't see why you felt the need to hurt yourself. It was not right for Ruth and James to see anything like that," she said in an uncharacteristically stern voice.

Evelyn could not believe that her normally quiet and reserved child challenged her. But she wanted Faith to understand her reasons, so she tried again. "That does not do justice to the punishment deserved. Do you not understand what it is like to stand before a holy God? Not one speck of sin in His past, present, or future. The embodiment of perfection! The intelligence to make the greatest earthly moment look absolutely ridiculous! Power! Power that your mind cannot even begin to comprehend. No eyes have ever witnessed such a deity! Do you have the slightest clue what we are up against? He hates sin! He hates lukewarm! He spits it out of his mouth! He hates sin so much that he sent his own son to die for it! What do you think he is going to do to you when you are face to face with him?!"

The moment was tense, the air that filled the room felt strained and thick, and nerves were wound so tight that it felt like they could snap and burst out of the skin. Evelyn had a look of uninhibited rage stamped over her face, and her eyes watered. But Faith looked right into her eyes and started to speak,

"I do not believe it works that way. I don't see Him wanting you to hurt yourself. This does not feel like love, Mama. It feels like guilt. It feels like fear. I was locked in a pitch-black basement for an average grade on a report card. James had no gifts for his birthday, and he had his money taken from him. Now you're burning yourself on the kitchen stove. I love you, Mama, I worry about you, and I never set out to defy you, but this does not feel right. I just..."

Smack!

Evelyn drew her hand back as far as she could and slapped Faith across the face. The impact was so powerful that it caused Faith to hit her head on the wall. The girl fell back with too much of a rush to notice any sort of pain, looking at her mother with pure shock struck across her face.

"You will learn to honor me! I will not let you talk to me like this! I am your mother! You do not have any clue what path you are walking towards! I will not have this! I will not take this disrespect!" Evelyn raged on and on.

With Faith still silent, holding her face in shock, Evelyn paced around the room, restless. At last, she seemed to make up her mind about something. Quickly, she walked to the trashcan next to the desk upon which Faith sat to do her homework and pulled away from it the plastic bag. She made her way to the bookshelf and started to pull the books off, filling the bag. When the bag was full, she kept pulling them off and let them pile onto the floor.

Sure enough, the only book she left was the Holy Bible. Snatching the sacred book from the shelf, Mama marched aggressively towards the bed and shoved it into Faith's chest.

"This is the only book you will be reading from now on. I will give these other books back when you start to bear fruit! Right now your fruit is rotten, but not for good," said Mama angrily before she stormed out of the room.

Evelyn nearly pulled her bedroom door off of the hinges when she flung it open. The Bible verses on her door fluttered, caught in the burst of wind of the slamming door, and fell to the floor. Alone again, she paced her messy room back and forth, ripping chunks out of her hair again, screaming in frustration. When at last she finally stopped her relentless walking, she fell into banging her head over and over again against the wall. Tears fell down her face as she shook uncontrollably.

Anger consumed her. There was too much anger inside of her frail body waiting to burst out! So, it only made sense to be destructive. Evelyn punched at her walls until they were painted with blood. Even with her knuckles torn open and throbbing with pain, it was not enough. Almost frantic, she walked to her dresser and pulled out a tiny razor blade.

Pulling her pants down past her knees, she held the blade to the side of her inner thigh. "I deserve punishment!" said Evelyn as she began to slice, punctuating each accusation against herself with a deep cut to her flesh. "I deserve wrath! I am wretched! I am dirty! I am unclean! I am a sinner!" The blood ran down her legs just as the tears flowed down her face. The scene would no doubt be horrific to anyone who could see it-- a skinny woman crying upon the floor, messy hair draped down and covering her face, blood streaming down her legs to pool onto the floor with endless tears.

"I am so sorry I failed you, Father. I am so sorry. I was never fit to be a daughter, and I am not fit to be a mother. I probably didn't even inflict the proper punishment on myself for my wrongdoings! I feel so worthless like I can't do anything right. How could I ever please you, Jesus? How could you ever use a wretched sinner like me? I can never amount to anything! Please, Jesus! Take this thorn out of my flesh and cover me in the blood of your righteous son, Jesus Christ. Give me your spirit. Change my heart, Lord. Make me a better person, and help me be a better mother. I do not want my children to live a life of sin! I am so sorry that I don't make you proud. I am sorry to be wicked! I do not understand how I can know what I want to do, yet I do not do them! Please have mercy on my soul, Lord!"

It was a tragic day in the Singleton household. With David at work, the other three children were left to worry about their mother. Faith sat against her wall for the longest time, holding the left side of her face in shock, her mind unable to process what had happened. Yet, not a single tear left her eye. James buried himself further into the make-believe adventures of his comic book, and Ruth went to her journal to reflect.

Evelyn wrapped her leg with a towel to stop the bleeding. She cried silently and prayed herself to sleep...

Chelsea was fourteen years old when she was impregnated by a popular football jock from the local high school. It all happened when she was invited to a sleepover by some of the popular girls in her school. Chelsea was a very pretty girl, but she only had a couple of friends. None of them were part of the popular crowd because they were believers in Jesus Christ, and so was she, though her family did not attend church regularly.

Chelsea's family read the Bible, and even though their house was not covered in Biblical decorations, they lived it out in their daily lives. The love they had for each other was a reflection of the time each put into their prayers, readings, and devotions. Outside of her family, Chelsea had two close friends who shared her convictions. They talked about Jesus, they didn't party, they were just trying to take it day by day the right way.

But Chelsea befriended some of the popular girls from her grade. Chelsea was an exceptional girl because she was loving towards everyone and always carried herself with humility. It was not hard to like someone like her. So, she made new friends, but she never turned her back on the two friends she already had, though she found herself talking to her new friends pretty often. She never shared Jesus with them, just her love.

On the night of the sleepover, the parents of the girl hosting the party were not home, having made weekend plans elsewhere. The popular girls invited a lot of people, and for the first time ever, Chelsea found herself in a party environment. Within the hour of the party's start, high schoolers were filling up the space with alcohol. Everybody was drinking, dancing, and having a good time. She felt uncomfortable, but she did not want to look dumb in front of anyone. So, she gave in to the peer pressure and joined the party.

There was a high school football jock that kept looking at her all night. She was flattered by the attention because she was immediately very attracted to him. He was almost three years older than her. It did not take long for him to approach her and ask her to dance. After they danced for a few minutes, they had some drinks. Everybody at the party was hooking up with each other and drinking nonstop. Things around the house were getting broken, and everybody was having the time of their lives. Halfway through the night, the boy whispered in Chelsea's ear for her to come upstairs with him, and she said yes.

She was very nervous going up the stairs with him, but even more nervous when she found herself in a bedroom alone with him all alone. But, she liked him and did not want to embarrass herself, so she pretended to be confident and certain. He kissed her, and she kissed him back. He kissed her harder, and he would not stop. She told him to stop. When that did not work, she screamed for him to stop. And nobody could hear her over the loud music downstairs

A few weeks later, she found out she was pregnant. The football jock was, by then, doing time for a sexual assault charge. That meant Chelsea was left alone to make a very difficult decision. Should she keep the baby? Chelsea and her parents felt like this baby could be a gift from God. That this child may grow up to do amazing things. The baby didn't have a voice, and they felt it was right to give it a chance to live. It was a child birthed out of a horrific sin, but they knew Jesus could redeem the moment. They were excited to bring the child up in love.

It was summertime when she had the baby, and she was going to be homeschooled so that she could be a stay at home mother. Every once in awhile, Chelsea left the house to attend a girls church group with her true friends, having rid herself of the popular girls. She wasn't into church, but she loved this group. Not one person judged her for being a teen mom. In fact, they actually offered her help.

Chelsea would hold her baby girl and marvel at her beauty. She knew her child came from a hurtful place, but she was like a radiant sunflower blooming out of the dirt. Chelsea could not wait to spend her days loving and protecting her daughter. Nobody would ever hurt you, Chelsea would whisper against the sleeping baby's soft cheek, mommy is right here.

But one morning after her parents left for work, she came out of the shower and walked into a nightmare. Her baby was gone! Her heart sank into her chest, dizzy and disbelieving. In a panic, she took very hard and quick breaths but still felt breathless. Like she was drowning, suffocating. Tears flowed out of her pretty blue eyes like a river. She fell into a state of panic and called the cops.

A year later, Chelsea still wasn't the same. She could not even enjoy her sweet sixteen. There was no peace in her heart or mind, just a heavy burden. She cried every night and carried in herself the heavy guilt of a parent who lost their child. How could someone take her baby in her own house? The thought of the unknown haunted her with every passing minute. Who has my child? What terrible things are being done to my baby? Is she crying for her mommy? Is she even alive?

Nothing took the pain away. Her parents couldn't help her, she stopped going to the girl's group, and she stopped praying altogether. She was hopeless. One morning, a few weeks after Chelsea turned sixteen, her parents woke up ready and determined to do something together as a family to heal. They knew it was a rough year for all of them, no one more than their distraught daughter, and they wanted happy moments again. After they made breakfast, they walked into Chelsea's room and found her dead body on the floor, an empty orange prescription pill bottle next to her fingers.

Chapter 6
4 a.m.

It had been nearly two months since the dramatic incident where Evelyn burned herself on the stove as punishment for being a bad mother. Life was tense for everyone in the Singleton household except Ruth and Evelyn. Everyone walked on eggshells. Evelyn had been erratic lately, her moods unpredictable and passionate. No one even dared speak for fear that Evelyn would find some way to trap them in their words.

It could be something simple like a public figure on television. Mama's opinions of superstars were very random and without a distinguishable pattern. Some would earn her approval by being like-minded. Some were regular people who made mistakes, and she would speak about them with so much grace. Mama would tell the children that the person behind the eyes was broken, someone who wanted to have a relationship with Jesus but had too many demands from Hollywood. She would mute the TV and begin to pray for the public figure, insisting that her children stop what they were doing to do the same.

But then there would be celebrities who appeared to be more positive than the ones she prayed for, yet she spoke about them with anger and frustration.

"A false prophet, children! She speaks lies into the ears of our youth! This is why all the kids at your school are so wicked! It is a good thing that this is your last week of school! You could be led astray," Evelyn would say with venom in her voice.

She broke into frequent rants about the influence of Pop culture: "This is a world of broken people who come from broken homes. They grew up abused, ignored, bullied, insecure, and many other wicked ways. Many are without parents, and many are without love. They have no one to follow, no model to imitate, we have Jesus and they have whoever the media tells them to follow. The children of today are raised by the media!"

Of course, when Mama disliked somebody on television, all of her children had to hate this person, as well. It was easier to go along with Mama than to fight her.

She often bragged about the letters that she sent to the celebrities she disliked. "I sent a letter to the Ellen show today, children! She keeps claiming to spread a message of love into the world, but her message of love does not have Christ at the center! I gave her a piece of my mind today, and I can't wait for her to be confronted! As long as the lie has a tiny bit of truth mixed in with it, anything can appear to be the truth. Homosexuality is an abomination, it says it in His word. Consider the source. Where is this message of love truly coming from? It comes from the mouth of a woman who believes love is love, even when our God is displeased with who she chooses to love. So what can she really teach you about love? Nothing!"

David wouldn't even watch TV with his family anymore. He had been annoyed for most of his life because everything had to be spiritual when he was never spiritual. He knew that none of the letter's recipients would ever read a crazy woman's hate letter! If they did by some chance, there was no chance they would respond. If anything, he loved the idea of Ellen giving them a call. Maybe she could interview his mother and expose her craziness to the world.

The daily and nightly devotionals were more difficult these days, as well. Nobody was ever able to be right about anything. Even when they kept their answers simple, it just was not correct. Evelyn started to have a very disagreeable spirit about her.

One night, James talked about the book of James, about how it was important to build people up, and how words can either bring people down or encourage them. Mama was disappointed in what he had to say about it. "People today do not need to have their hand held in the world. They need to be confronted with the wickedness of their evil ways!" seethed Evelyn.

No one was immune. On the same night, Ruth discussed a devotional about confronting people in their sin. But Mama had an angry response for that, as well, and yelled at them all. "Nobody will ever come to Jesus if they feel attacked! This is why we don't have believers anymore! This is why people leave the church! You are going to be judged by the same measure you pass judgment onto others!"

Mama was becoming more difficult to live with, and so was Ruth. The youngest of the Singleton children had always carried herself in a know-it-all sort of way, but it was growing worse. Nobody was able to say anything to her either. It was crazy to David especially because Evelyn never allowed Ruth to be right about anything either. Did Ruth even realize her mother was becoming a mean person?

Ruth acted like the Singleton household hall monitor, stomping her way from room to room, making sure everybody was doing their devotionals. She was snappy towards her siblings and quick to set them straight. "Don't eat until Mama cooks! No Ellen on the TV! This commercial for that new scary movie will invite demonic spirits! Switch the channel now!" she would order with a bratty expression.

Everybody had to move together as a family, as well. They all went to the grocery store, they all went for a drive; anywhere Evelyn had to be, so did her kids. She was even more disrespectful towards people outside of their house than she was her own children. She seemed like she was always bracing for confrontation with people. There was one person who was following her car too close and ended up at the same gas station as them. Mama marched her way to the person and began to give him a piece of her mind. The children could only catch certain words, but it entertained them to see her pointing her finger in his chest.

She would complain to management everywhere they went as well. All hell broke loose one day they stopped to eat at Burger King. Evelyn complained to management and insisted that they give her and her children their food for free. "That man in the back making our burgers has a cough!" yelled Evelyn, drawing the attention of the establishment's few patrons who stopped eating to stare at the spectacle.

"Okay?" said the manager.

"Well, who knows how many burgers that nasty delinquent may have coughed all over!" she retorted loudly.

Like his older brother, James was annoyed by their Mama. But, he also envied the control that she had over the people around her. He was just a scared, quiet, little boy. As tiny as his mother was, her personality was large and abrasive. She had no fear of anyone, she had no care for the feelings of the ones she squared off against, and people were intimidated by her. At times, James wished he could have this type of personality. Mama was always the dominant force in the conversation.

As annoying as Mama could be, it was something James thought about. What if he could control people the way Mama could? What if he intimidated people like she did? He would have power over people, and that was a thought that sparked his interest. But, he knew he was too introverted to ever be this way or possess those traits.

It was embarrassing to be anywhere with Mama in public. Ruth was the only one who seemed unbothered by Mama's behavior. In fact, she loved every minute of it. She felt proud that Mama was running things inside and outside of the house. But, she did not seem to notice that her mother was not as sweet towards her as she used to be.

Mama also came off as overbearing to strangers because she had to evangelize to everybody. She would walk up to a random person and see them as if they had a 'save me' sign on their back. Daily, she confronted people about their sins and slights.

"Excuse me, sir," she asked one man recently, accosting him outside of a department store, "but have you ever lied before? Have you ever stolen? Have you ever been attracted to another woman other than your wife?"

"Umm, yes to all these things. What is this? A survey?"

"Well, that makes you a liar, a thief, and an adulterer! You are knees deep in sin and the only way out is Jesus Christ!"

This approach had never once worked.

The most annoying part for David was riding in the car with her. He already viewed her as crazy, fake, cruel, and evil, so hearing her sing worship made his hatred for her rise to new heights. She would sing very loudly and off pitch, raise her arm to the top of the car, and sing her praises. She had to be bold, and she had to sing louder than the music in the car. He hated this because it was all for show. She just wanted to show them how holy she was. Look at me kids, look at how close to Jesus I am! You guys have a long way to go. It just never came across as genuine to David. So, he would sigh and try his best to tune her out.

To make matters worse, she was upset with herself because she had to reach out to her rich parents for support. It was nothing for them to pay off any bills she needed help with, but it killed her to ask them for help. The loud crying behind her bedroom door grew more obvious to everyone in the house. Glass could be heard breaking, poundings on the walls sounded through the house, and her always guilt-driven prayers were coming in at full effect.

She hated needing their money, though her parents seemed to have no problem sending it over. Of course, David knew it had to be hard for Evelyn to ask the parents that she never saw or took her children to meet for anything. Evelyn always said it was only until she got back on her feet, but nobody ever saw her look for a job. Her parents weren't even rushing her for a job.

David understood the causes of the tension between Evelyn and her parents were unknown to him and his siblings, but he could tell that they were always at odds with each other. Evelyn never seemed happy when they called her. In fact, she hardly picked up when they called. When she did talk to them, she always spent the next couple hours of the day angry. Even when her parents were sending money, she never seemed to like them.

He did wonder if they had anything to do with why Evelyn was the way she was. It was truly crazy to think that he and his siblings hardly knew their own grandparents. Maybe there was a reason for that. But, the idea of Evelyn's parents being worse than her was hard to fathom, though it was also highly possible.

Tomorrow was the last day of school. David could not believe how quickly the last few months had flown by. It normally worked that way. Whenever you want the days to go by slowly, they go by so quickly. Whenever you want the days to go by quickly, they go by too slow. He loved school because that was seven hours or more away from life at home. After school, he had his shifts at the movie theater to keep him away even more. But now he would have to be around his crazy mother twice as much.

For his siblings, he imagined it was not as much torture for them. They were on the same page as her, and they didn't seem to view her as a hypocrite. The religious-themed days held purpose to them, while to him, they were lies. Evelyn didn't have a job anymore, so she would be at the house all day. He dreaded going to bed the night before that last school day. It meant he would have his last seven hours of freedom from his mother.

That night, he laid on his bed looking at the ceiling, anxiety starting to settle in his chest and stomach, making him feel heavy and sick. He felt like he was out of time. He applied to many different colleges and universities in preparation for the last day of high school. He wanted to attend a university nearby so that he could still see his brother and sisters, though he planned to live on campus. But he would be willing to take any way out at this point. He even applied to Liberty University, and this was the last resort for him because it was a Christian based college. He said what he had to on the application to hopefully convince the admissions board to accept him.

He just wanted to get away, and tomorrow was the last day of school but no acceptance letters had come. Even if they did, David worried about the outcome of his mother finding one of those letters. She was excited for him to be done with school. She was very anti-secular education lately. She had no trust in the school system and the people that her children interacted with in public school. It was bad enough that no church was righteous enough for her, but now going to school was an issue. Everything was starting to look evil in her eyes, yet she walked out of the house with boldness and confidence like she was going to get the best of the world before it got the best of her.

What did she really expect of him anyway? Did she really think her children would be with her forever? That he wouldn't go out into the world with aspirations of bettering himself? That Faith and Ruth would never get married and have a family of their own? That James would never venture off into the world and maybe create his own superheroes? There was never any talk of what comes after high school, and there was never any talk of leaving home. David felt like this was something most parents talked to their kids about before the last day of school. It made him nervous that it was never talked about.

As his thoughts ran wild, he could hear the crying from behind his thin walls. It was hard to make out the words, but he could make out the voice. It was Evelyn. She is really losing her mind, he thought to himself. He reached over towards his lamp and switched the light off. As he laid down in the dark silence, he closed his eyes and fell into a deep sleep.

David was woken up by violent knocks on his bedroom door. As he slowly began to wake up his thoughts felt scrambled. He felt like too much was happening at the same time-- the noise, his lack of awareness, and the fact he was still very tired. He looked over at the clock next to his bed and saw that it was 4 a.m. Before he could take a breath and answer the door, Evelyn barged through his door and stormed into his room.

"Wake up, David! Wake up! Living room, now!" she said aggressively.

If he was fully awake, he would think she had at last gone fully crazy, but he was too tired to ponder any thoughts in his head at this moment in time. He sat up as quickly as he could and got out of bed. His body felt weak from his lack of sleep, and he yawned with nearly every step towards the living room. But each step roused him awake enough to wonder what this was all about by the time he entered the living room..

    James, Faith, and Ruth were all sitting on the couch already by the time he arrived. They each looked half-awake and unsure of why they were being summoned so early before the last day of school. Evelyn made a gesture towards David that let him know the empty spot at the end of the couch was for him, so he casually filled in the spot.

    Evelyn was pacing the living room like a madwoman. After a few tense seconds, she finally came to a stop. When she did, she looked at her four children and began to speak with an undoubted charisma.

    "I am sure you are all wondering why you are here this early. Well, you are all awake because, according to Matthew 18:15-17, I need two or three witnesses for what is about to take place. James, listen up."

    As soon as James heard his name he nervously looked up at Mama. She took a good silent look at him, nodded to herself, and began to speak expressively.

"James, I am not happy with the grades you have received this year. They are unacceptable. I feel like I have made many points about the importance of excellence, but you are so unresponsive."

David felt anger boil inside, and he knew this was not going to end well for his brother. Both Ruth and Faith had blank nervous expressions on their faces. James remained quiet as Mama continued her lecture.

"I named you after the book of James for a special reason. I feel like the wisdom in those few pages are more precious than gold. I had enough faith in my Lord to claim intelligence over your life. So, I have to ask why you don't display this wisdom? What is your excuse? Your brother and sisters are all straight-A students. Yet you get C's and D's on your papers. All year I've heard from your teachers that you have some kind of learning disability. But maybe I have been wrong to be so easy on you. I should expect excellence from you. So what do you have to say for yourself?"

James remained silent under the inquisition, looking downward at the floor. But David spoke up for his brother, "Mom, this..."

"Be quiet! I asked him! Let him speak!" yelled Mama harshly.

David found himself quiet and surprised, shocked that he shut himself up so naturally when she commanded.

Mama looked at James and asked, "So? What do you have to say for yourself? Why are your grades not reflecting excellence? Why should you get a special pass in this family? Are you more special than your siblings?"

Still, James remained quiet, tears falling down his face, too afraid to speak.

"Hmm, well, maybe everything you own in your bedroom can be taken away until you give me an answer," said Evelyn sarcastically.

David looked over at his sisters and realized they had not moved a muscle. James was silently crying, too afraid to look Mama in the eyes. David took a soft breath and spoke up. "Mom, just wait..."

"Shut up David!" Evelyn yelled in a fit of rage.

Once again David froze up, fear settling in. It made no sense to him that it was so natural to fall into compliance. He was bigger, too grown up to be physically hurt by her, but something must have triggered. He looked away from her towards the hallway.

Evelyn, like a mean witch, moved closer to James until she was directly in his personal space.

She quietly and slowly crouched down until her face was leveled with his. She said, "Look at me son."

But James couldn't do it, his eyes remained glued to the floor, and his shirt was covered in tears. Evelyn rolled her eyes, grabbed a giant handful of his hair, and aggressively pulled his head up so he would look her dead in the eyes. "I said look at me!" Are you just too stupid to give me an answer? Is that it? Are your teachers actually telling me the truth? You are stupid!"

James held his mother's hands as they firmly gripped his hair and he cried out, "No!"

She screamed in his face louder and asked, "Do you need me to speak slower? Should I spell things out for you? Can you even spell? I mean, you are stupid after all, that is the reason why you can't bring me decent grades!"

David had enough. The rage that had been boiling inside him had found its way out like a horse that broke free from its fenced barriers. His nerves felt like they had burst out of his chest as he quickly stood to his feet. "That's enough Mom!" he yelled authoritatively.

She let go of James's hair and turned her attention to David. "Oh wow, look who all of a sudden has a voice now," said Evelyn sarcastically. She slowly walked closer to David, clapping her hands in what seemed like slow motion. Before he knew it, she was in his personal space now.

"I needed two or three witnesses to affirm my decision for punishing one of you. But it looks like I will need to remind you who is in charge," said Evelyn.

David was full of anger and adrenaline, and he knew he would have to take advantage of this feeling in order to speak his mind. "Mom, you are crazy. Seriously, do you really think this is right? Just take a step back and look at all of this!" he yelled.

Evelyn's palms were shaking uncontrollably, her breathing was far more forced, and tears were falling down her face in frustration. She drew herself so far into David's space that she was almost budding heads with him, and she looked dead into his eyes. But as nervous as he was, he looked back into hers. The younger siblings were locked into the intense moment that was unfolding before them. They were nervous for their brother, did not know what to make of Mama, but remained silent.

Evelyn, in a tone of pure hatred, said, "I bet you feel so big. So, so, so big. That's just great for you! Well, it does not matter how you feel because I am going to let you in on a little secret. You are too small for me!"

She had screamed her last sentence so loud that even brave David flinched. He never broke eye contact, but even he was holding back tears.

"You are still that pathetic sad little boy, who reminded me of his sorry pitiful father that I hated so much," said Evelyn harshly but quietly. "I was really hoping, praying, that I beat some kind of sense into you. But here we are and you want to defy me!"

He looked at her intently and said, "You are damn right. I am done. So done with all of this. You are absolutely nuts and you don't fool me."

"You are so blasphemous! You better pray to your Lord for forgiveness when I am done with you, David! You need to find yourself humbly at the feet of the cross! How dare you! Know your place! I am your mother! He commands you to honor me!" yelled Evelyn ballistically.

"Your God does not exist!" David yelled back. It was like time itself stopped, and silence pierced the atmosphere. Everybody in the room stared at David with their mouths wide open. Ruth, Faith, and James all had tears running down their cheeks. Evelyn just looked irate.

He realized with surprising clarity that he started something that could not be undone, but he felt too proud and too frustrated to lie anymore. David took a deep breath and began to speak. "I don't believe in this. I never did. But nobody can even talk to you. What God would want this? Even if he made a little bit of sense to me, what God would want this? Being forced to read this book every day, which is written by other flawed people by the way! Being forced to pray, nothing is our decision, it's all you! No church was ever good enough for you, Mom! How many have we left over the years? There comes a point where you have to see the problem is you! Nobody likes you, or gets along with you! That's why we don't go to church! That's why nobody in our family ever comes to see us! That is why we never see them! Because to you, nobody but you gets to be right! Nobody can ever have a different opinion, even when it has to do with this God that you believe in! A God that is a part of a man-made religion that has so many holes in it! You are literally the worst human being I have ever met in my life! So how good is this God then anyways? If the best I can be with him is anything like you, then it's just not worth it! It's no wonder your mom and dad hate you!"

    In the heat of the intense moment, Evelyn swung in a fit of rage at David's face. But David somehow caught her punch and held her fist. "That will be the last time you ever hit me," he said with pure hatred in his voice. He let go of her fist and started to slowly make his way to the front door.

Evelyn stood still, shaking in anger with her messy hair covering the front of her face. "It is almost five o'clock in the morning, where are you going?" she said.

"I am going to finish out my last day of school peacefully, then find somewhere else to live," said David.

"You'll come back," said Evelyn sarcastically.

"No Mom, I have a lot of options, and they are all better than this. I will eventually end up in college and far away from you," he replied.

Evelyn began to silently laugh menacingly as she watched her son begin to open the front door. " Just like your father! A coward! Walking away from conflict, walking away from your problems! Turning your back on family! You are just like him!" she roared.

David paused, ready to snap back at her until Ruth screamed across the room. "Don't say anything! Just leave! You are dishonoring your Earthly mother, you give no acknowledgment to the God who made you, and you have lied to us our whole lives! We looked up to you and wanted faith like yours! But it was never real, to begin with! Mama is right! You are a coward and you should leave just like he did!" shrieked Ruth as tears streamed down her reddened face.

David felt crushed, absolutely devastated, to hear this from his littlest sister. He looked at Faith and asked, "Well?" But she just remained quiet with her eyes to the floor. He nodded okay to himself with heavy sorrow in his heart. He took a breath and looked at James. But his younger brother just kept his head down like Faith. "You guys think this is normal, but it's not normal! She is not right! There is no God and you don't have to live like this!" yelled David.

"Just go!" shouted Ruth.

"So what now? You continue a life of forced Bible studies and prayers? You go on forever never having a voice of your own? You burn and punish yourself whenever you sin? You deal with this crazy woman who needs to be on her meds? Look at everything she has done! If God was real, she does not have this right!" yelled David.

"Leave!" screamed Ruth.

Evelyn looked at her oldest son with disgust. She knew the other children were on her side and had faith in her. She was able to crack a smile because of this thought. She said with a powerful finality, "You go do whatever it is you have to do."

He looked back at his mother with hate in his eyes and replied, "it's about time I did."

The front door slammed with David's exit and only soft crying could be heard. Mama walked over to her three children and embraced them with a loving hug. "Everything is going to be okay, I am so proud of you guys. I know that was hard, but you had so much faith. James, don't even worry about anything, you are not in trouble anymore."

They all cried together for a while, united in a circle. Reassured of the faith they displayed, they each were sent off to get ready for their last day of school.

As James returned to his bedroom, he began to go through his closet for clothing to wear to school. He felt so much rage welling inside of him. How could his own mother treat him this way? He hated being called stupid, it was humiliating to him. All because things were difficult for him to understand. He didn't pick up on things as quickly as the other kids did in class, and he was always the one that seemed a few steps behind. Teachers already talked to him slower than the other kids. He was immediately taken back to all of the moments when the other kids saw someone treat him like he was stupid. As creative as his imagination could be, he just didn't understand why everything else was so difficult to understand.

If only he could be the dominant force in a situation the way that Mama always was. In his head,

James visualized telling her to shut her mouth when she began to insult him. He saw her in a corner crying her eyes out because of the verbal abuse he inflicted on her. He saw her trying to scream at him and being shut down when he talked over her. He imagined a world where he wasn't afraid of her but she was afraid of him. He even imagined being smarter than her. She always had some sort of comeback, but not with him. He wanted to be sharper in the mind. He wanted her to feel stupid the way he did.

But that thought was quickly dismissed when he came to a realization of the harsh reality that he lived in. He was not Evelyn. He was quiet, shy, always at a loss for words, and, most importantly, he was weak. Nobody ever crossed his mother, and nobody was ever able to step into her world and tell her how it worked. It was probably best for him to bury these thoughts as deep as he could because they were nothing but wishful thinking. What would he be without his brother?

David was gone now.

Who was here to protect him and cheer him up when Evelyn took away his belongings? He not only felt rage towards his mother, but he was beginning to feel anger towards David.

How could David leave him?

Chapter 7
The Encounter

David got into his car as quickly as he could after he stormed out. It was so early in the morning that it was still dark outside. He got into the driver's seat, started the car, and then sat back frozen to recapture the moment that just happened. Before he knew it, he began to tear up and shake with anger, then started to scream as loud as he could. Not even that eruption subdued the force of anger in him, and he pounded the steering wheel over and over again screaming uncontrollably. It felt like stress with his heartbeat physically pounding it's way out of his body from all angles. He had no control, completely blacked out with rage.

After he screamed and pounded out his anger, he drove off.

As he started to focus on driving, he felt both of his hands pulsating with pain and heat. Looking down, he saw that his knuckles were bleeding, but he was able to move all of his fingers, which was a very good sign. At least he knew his hands were not broken.

As he focused on the road ahead, he couldn't help but think it was really stupid of him to beat his car up.

He had no idea where he was going to go. School didn't start for another two hours, but he couldn't go home. Because he had nowhere and nothing, he drove through the neighborhoods of his county, allowing his mind to run free.

It seemed like with every passing streetlight or building he had another flashback of his miserable life at home. Memories flickered through his head in scattered and jumbled form. It eventually dawned on him that all his possessions were at the house, so he would have to set foot in it sooner or later. A half an hour into his mindless wandering, he stopped at a 24-hour pancake house that was minutes away from his school and parked his car.

David wasn't hungry. As a matter of fact, he couldn't eat anything even if he tried. He felt too many nerves all at once, his stomach in knots, and he just wanted to relax. So, he set his seat back as far as it could go so that he could lay back and stare at the roof of his car.

He could not believe what was happening. He was hoping he would be able to find a place to stay. Maybe one of his close friends would allow him to stay with them for the summer until he figured out what he was going to do with himself. He began to feel a lot of anxiety about the unknown, he wondered if he had just made the biggest mistake of his life.

His mind still rang with the sound of his mother saying, "you'll be back," and it replayed over and over. He wanted nothing more than to prove her wrong by never needing her for anything. He was ready to be a man and fend for himself.

Relaxed and no longer focused on the road, his hands began to throb worse, and he reached into his glove department and grabbed some napkins he had saved from Starbucks. He held them over the wounds and was thankful the scrapes weren't too bad. He was calming down somewhat now that he focused on things other than what his mind wanted to ceaselessly replay. It would have been for nothing if he broke his hands in a fit of rage.

Despite everything, he was also worried about his siblings. What would happen to them? He felt it in his gut that they would experience the cycle of abuse he used to have with Evelyn. She was on her medication their entire lives, but he alone knew what she was like without it. Though she did have a much different relationship with his siblings, and he found some kind of comfort in the idea that only he would ever get the worst of it. It made him sick that they didn't know half of what Evelyn was truly capable of. They were innocent children and knew no better.

This is how they were raised.

It was normal to do Bible studies before anything, to interpret what they read at a young age, to be expected perfection, to hate celebrities they will never meet, to carry the weight of guilt and beg their savior to forgive them for every little thing, to be the only family with the truth, to never be able to outsmart their mother, to be yelled at, to be punished.

He sighed to himself and found sorrow in the thought that they would never know what normal was until they were away from Evelyn. Because she was their mother, she was all they knew, she could never be wrong.

Maybe Faith was old enough and smart enough to question all of it, but Ruth was sold on everything. This meant that James most likely leaned towards what the norm was for him growing up. The norm for his brother and sisters was crazy for David. That was always the truth that divided him from his younger brother and sisters.

What if they were all right? What if he was a coward? He hated the thought of being anything like his father because he hated his father, and buried any thought that there might be even the smallest similarity. How long did any of them expect him to live under his mother's care anyway? He was not a husband or a father, he was a brother. He has no obligation to live somewhere he did not want to live. His little sister Ruth made it very clear that she didn't want him there, and Faith and James didn't even stand up for him. There would be time to say proper goodbyes whenever he was ready to collect his belongings.

Beneath the doubt and anxiety, David had to admit that it felt so good to put his mom in her place. To finally have a voice; not just any voice either, but his! He meant every word, and he refused to go on pretending anymore. To him, God didn't exist. He wasn't going to waste any more of his time pretending to believe in something he would never wrap his mind around. He prided himself on being intelligent, and that was the whole point. He was too smart to believe in this.

He had more questions than answers, no peace about what he had read all these years, and the product of this religion was someone like his crazy mother. He wished that he was never quiet, that he had been honest from the start.

He just lay back in the seat of his car until his phone alarm went off. It was time to finish up his last day of school.

As he drove, it kind of bummed him out that nobody would show up to his graduation. As of that moment, his family was no longer on good terms with him. He looked like a traitor. Graduation was going to take place tomorrow. Many schools normally had graduation before the last day of school, but he liked that his was after. It was exciting to think that tomorrow he would walk across the stage in glory.

As he pulled into Grafton High School, it looked like a celebration.

His fellow seniors who were also graduating had the windows of their cars written on and decorated. There were glorious banners hanging out of the school windows and everybody was hanging outside of the school. The atmosphere was positive and vibrant.

As soon as he parked his car and started to make his way into the school, everybody high fived him on the way in. He looked like the most popular guy in school. It felt great, but he was really just anxious to see his friends.

He walked through the hallway on his way to Ms. Kellbrook's classroom when he heard someone singing Blink 182 behind him. He turned around and immediately knew it was Travis.

"What's up to David!" Travis asked enthusiastically.

"Nothing much. Got in a giant fight with my mother and now I don't have a place to live."

Travis looked back at his friend with a puzzled look on his face and said, "Sorry to hear that, bro. Maybe you can stay at my place until you figure something out."

"Man, I would really love that. Please ask your parents and let me know what they say."

"Sure thing," said Travis.

"So where are Michael and Jason?" asked David. Travis casually responded by saying that Michael was somewhere around the school and Jason didn't see any point in attending the last day of school.

David talked to Travis outside of the classroom for a while about movies and music, each second separating him more and more from the events of last night. This was always the main connection between them. It was like their separate language. Nobody saw the same movies or knew the same bands they did.

"Blink 182 is not Blink 182 anymore!" yelled Travis with a lot of passion in his voice. "Tom Delonge left the band to form his stupid alien group, and Matt Skiba took his place. They are too old, they are forty-year-old men trying to act like they're still in their twenties! They can't even sing anymore. I mean, even if Tom came back, he hates singing punk music. Blink would just end up being a crappier version of Angels and Airwaves!"

"I kind of like Angels and Airwaves, Travis," said David nervously.

"That's because you freaking suck!" shouted Travis as he walked towards his class in the opposite direction.

David laughed off the moment and was excited to get through this last day of school. He was about to step foot into Ms. Kellbrook's classroom when he caught sight of Michael leaning against a locker on the opposite hallway. David began to walk towards his direction to see him before class. When he made his way to Michael, he found him just relaxing like the cool hipster he was.
"What's up, dude," said Michael as mellow as you could greet someone.
"Not much man, about to finish up class," replied David.
Michael looked like he was pondering a thought as he stared off into space. He finally looked at David and said, "Lame, bro. How about we skip class and hang outside."
It didn't sound like a bad idea at all because classes were pretty much done already. All the work had been turned in, and there were no more assignments or tests due on the last day of school. It was always a half-day and the most mellow of all school days. So David agreed to skip the class and hang out with Michael.

As they casually snuck out of the building, Michael asked David how he was doing.

"If I'm honest with you, I'm doing terrible," David admitted.

"What's wrong?" Michael replied.

"I just got in a really big fight with my mom and now I don't have a place to live."

They found themselves outside and behind the school, near the open field where they found a patch of grass that appeared to be hidden from the windows where any teachers could spot them.

As they sat down, Michael started to talk. "You know man, it's crazy because as long as I have known you I've never heard you talk about your family. Honestly, we hang out every day at school. That's really it. We talk every day, but I still feel like I don't really know you all that well. I feel like you don't know me all that well, too."

"I'm sorry, bro, it's not on purpose, it just never came up," said David.

"Well, tell me about your family. Not trying to be weird or anything, just now I realized I have never once heard you mention them. I always talk about how my sister annoys me, that my mom did something awesome, or that my Dad showed me how to do something. So tell me something. Anything." said Michael happily. Openly.

"Well, where do I start?" David paused to think. "I have my younger brother James. Quiet kid who lives in his own little world. But he would probably talk your head off because he is a superhero and comic book fanatic."

"Comic books are freaking awesome bro! I always get told I look like Peter Parker," said Michael smoothly.

"Yeah. Right. Then I have a younger sister named Faith. She's the reader of the family. Ruth is my other sister, and she's a bratty know it all. There you go. That's my family."

Michael nodded his head and cautiously but casually asked, "And your dad?"

"He left," said David bluntly.

"Sorry, didn't mean to hit a nerve," said Michael.

"No, you didn't. It's okay. He left when I was a kid, he just couldn't put up with my mom."

Michael paid close attention and seemed interested in everything David told him. "Your mom is that bad, bro?"

"Yeah man, she really is."

"What makes her so bad?"

David smiled and said, "Wow, well, how much time you got buddy?"

They both burst into laughter. As soon as it calmed down Michael insisted on David describing his mother.

"Between us, because I am not proud of this, and I have known you for a while... I grew up with a mentally ill mother. She was terrible. My Dad was a very nice guy, a calm spirit, but he didn't have much of a backbone. My mom tore him apart on the daily. He couldn't say or do anything right. See, my mom is sick and she would get mad at him and take it out on me. I got beat a lot as a kid. My siblings grew up with a different version of her, a more stable her that stayed on her medication. But, my Dad eventually had enough of her and left. I really can't blame him either. I hate that woman so much. She claims to have this close relationship with Jesus, but she is such a terrible person. And my siblings these last few years are doing forced Bible studies, prayer hours, and theological discussions and debates. Christianity has been shoved down my throat."

Michael was completely tuned in, never breaking his eye contact. He had this empathetic look to him that didn't come off as someone who felt sorry for him. Now and then he would even nod his head in affirmation, showing that he was being an active listener.

It felt great for someone to just listen, for his words to actually matter, to feel safe with expressing himself. So he kept on talking.

"To my brother and sisters, they grew up this way, so it's the norm. We have been kicked out of so many churches and small groups, all because of my mom. Nobody gets along with her and she is never wrong. No doctrine is sound unless it comes from her crazy brain. She is so difficult to deal with. She hates everything and thinks it's evil, but she is evil. We were not allowed to disagree with her, so to avoid more hard living on top of hard living, I pretended to believe in all that stuff. But what I don't see is how my brother and sisters can't see how silly this is. Everything is harsh and over-the-top with my mom. She burned herself on a stove to punish herself for sin. She cries in her room all night and screams these guilt-driven prayers. Nothing is ever enough for her either. Religion has made her sickness so much worse. I can go on and on for days, man. Just please don't report this or say anything to anyone."

David didn't even realize he was shaking and holding back tears. He found it hard to remain composed and felt short of breath. He truly hated his mother with a burning passion and just wanted out. Not only out physically, but out mentally. She haunted his thoughts and he felt like he gave her too much power over his self-esteem. With a deep breath, David looked at Michael to see his reaction to everything he'd been told.

"Of course not," said Michael. He paused with a look that appeared to be in very deep thought. "Look, David... You're a really smart guy. One of the most thoughtful people I have ever met. If there's one thing I have gotten to know about you, it's that you're smart as hell."

"Well thanks, man, don't give me too much credit," said David.

The look on Michael's face started to take a more serious turn and then said, "Well, I think you're smart enough to know that Jesus is not the way you have seen him portrayed through your mother. If you really read the Gospel for yourself, which I assume you did, I mean you had to... Then you know there is so much grace. Your mother is sick, David. I promise you, He doesn't want you to be forced into a relationship with Him. He doesn't want you to live your life by a checklist, and he is not this stern father in the sky who is never proud of you, so the constant guilt for every little thing is not from Him. You don't have to punish yourself. You are not supposed to be at odds with every church or person who disagrees with you. You have to shine your own light and be a part of something. He made you unique and you have so much to offer that only you can offer.

David was a bit surprised because he had never seen Michael passionate or emotional about anything. As he said, you can only know and see so much in school. The faith that Michael spoke to him was real to him, this was something different than what he grew up with. It made sense to him what Michael said because the God he did read about sounded nothing like his mother's interpretation. He looked back at Michael and continued to listen.

"It's simple, very simple, bro... Love. Trust in His love for you. He already died for your sins, so there is no need to count them. Trust and believe what He did was enough to cover you. Then allow Him to change you at a pace that feels natural to you. He is not a God who says you need to clean up before you set foot in his presence. He is a God that wants you as you are, He wants a relationship with you, He wants to walk with you through everything. That's where the change comes from, dude. It will happen, you just have to let Him in. The real Him. Not this messed up version of Him that has been crammed down your throat."

David was mind blown, he never once heard it put this way. Michael never hid the fact he was a Christian, but he never once pressed his beliefs on anyone. This didn't even feel like someone pressing their beliefs. It seemed like a thought to consider.

"It's a lot more complicated than that. There is where the Bible came from, culture vs. scripture, and which is more important. Like, is it the Holy Spirit or my thoughts? What slavery and sexism in the Bible? It really gets complicated," said David.

But Michael just stared at him, smiled, and said, "No bro, it's not complicated at all. You are the one who's complicating it. Love. That's it. Love saved you, you are still loved, and your calling is to love. Deep down inside, you believe in that. You hate your mom, you hate God, but how can you hate someone so much if they don't exist to you? Just think about this. You're smart, really smart. Your faith does not need to be your mother's faith, it has to be your faith."

Michael seemed very passionate for the first time in their friendship. David was able to tell that this was something he longed to do. To express his faith and figure out where his friend stood when it came to it. "Look, man, if I died today, I wouldn't really care about people loving me for all I knew," said Michael. He stopped for a quick second to gather his thoughts and continued his stream of consciousness.

"When I die, I want nothing but love spoken over my casket. I want people to have stories for days about how I always treated them as if they were the most important people on Earth. People should have stories for days about the good deeds I have done for them out of the kindness of my heart. The woman in my life needs to see me as the one that got away. The friends who didn't stick around need to regret their decision. I want everyone to feel like I have impacted their life in a powerful way. When people ask why I was like this, someone can tell them Jesus made me this way. I love you because he loves me. I don't care about theology when people are killing themselves right now. I had a teenage girl cry in my arms at a public restaurant yesterday! All because nobody likes her posts on social media. She says it shows her that if she died, nobody would even notice. So seriously, bro! Forget all of that other stuff and just love people!"

    David stared at the patch of grass he was sitting on and pondered everything Michael said. He finally looked back up and said, "It's a lot to reflect on, but I will."

    They dropped the theological conversations and spent the next couple of hours goofing off and reflecting on senior year. They talked about graduation, what they hope to do after graduation, funny lunchtime memories, and about the pretty girls in the school they each had a crush on.

    They were only supposed to skip one class, but they found themselves with only thirty more minutes left of the last day of school when they finally stopped their conversations. So, they thought it would be a good idea to join the other students in the lobby.

Everybody was happy, signing each other's yearbooks, running all over the place, and taking pictures with each other. David and Michael caught up to Travis, who was excited to tell David he could stay with him for the summer, and they all hung out until the final bell rang.

They said their goodbyes and walked happily through the doors for the last time as students. David told Travis that he would drive home to get these belongings first, then meet him at his place. It was hard to not feel so blessed during times like these. When the friends you always had to be strong for were ready to be strong for you when it mattered most.

Before David could step out the door he heard Ms. Kellbrook's voice from behind him. "Skipped my class didn't you?"

He turned back around and smiled, then said, "We never do anything on the last day and you know it."

She smiled and replied, "True, but I know my favorite student was not about to just dip out of my classroom forever without saying his goodbyes."

David immediately walked up to her and gave her a giant hug. "I seriously enjoyed your class and I am going to miss you."

She continued to smile and broke into a mini-speech. "I see greatness in you David, I really do. Such a bright man and I can't help but notice a glow about you. I really believe that you won't only be great, but that you will go on to accomplish whatever it is you want to accomplish."

"I just want my life to be something special," said David. "The truth is, my only goal was to get into a college. But I really have no plans on what I am going to do when I get there. I want a dream, something that I can always chase. I feel like my life would be complete if there was something to live for, and dreams are always worth living for. Hopefully, it comes to me at some point, but I don't want my life amounting to a regular 9 to 5 dead-end job. People look miserable cleaning trash at the mall. Old men and women cleaning tables, it's not right. It makes me wonder if they ever had a dream and what happened to it. Were they too afraid to chase it? I don't know, I just want something I can love enough to put it all on the line for."

The look that Ms. Kellbrook gave him, as she did all her students, was an expression that any child wanted to receive from their parents. She didn't have to say anything because it was all in her face. She held back tears, and to no surprise had a response to what he said regarding dreams. "My dream was to have a student of mine see beyond what the world tells them they should. It brings me so much joy to see you longing for a dream. It is worth every second of breathing to live and die for a dream. I would rather live for my dream and possibly never achieve it than to die never trying. Imagine the burden of knowing there was so much that should have been done, but you were just too scared to try. Life is too short not to try. It is said that dreams are the language of God."

He felt breath taken by this, and it truly warmed his heart. He gave her another hug, said his thank-yous and goodbyes, then headed out the door.

As he walked through the parking lot to find his car, he felt happiness and a sense of accomplishment. He just graduated high school. He stuck it out through all the assignments, he studied for countless hours, and he stayed late on many occasions. He worked hard to get here and made it to the end. He had many good memories, and he only wished he could live in all these little moments forever. These days were golden and he only wished he didn't see them as regular school days.

He found his car and started it up. As soon as the engine rumbled to life, his feeling of happiness quickly turned into anxiety. He actually had to go back home. He needed to get his things and would most likely deal with Hell on Earth when he set foot in the house.

Every passing building meant being closer to his neighborhood, and his heart beat faster by the second.

What was going to happen when he walked into the house? Was his crazy mother going to throw plates at his head or something? Or maybe he would walk into her burning her other arm on the stove. He did defy her after all. Or even worse, what if he walked in and his brother and sisters hated him even more than they did when he walked out. What if he had to deal with hateful words?

As he drove on he began to wonder what school was like for them today. School had always been an escape for him because he had friends to go to. But they didn't have any friends as far as he knew. They really just kept to themselves. He hated the idea of his fight with Evelyn replaying in their minds all day. That was a good way to ruin the last day of school. He felt terrible inside, he did not want his siblings to hate him over this. They just didn't understand, they don't know that crazy lady the way they thought they did. She really was at best sick, and at worst evil.

He feared the negativity and what it would turn them into. He was able to see tiny glimpses of

Ruth becoming something terrible. James was so quiet, he may never break out of his shell. With a crazy mother constantly screaming at him and making him feel stupid, he could very well accept this identity. He didn't want his little brother to believe he was stupid. Because the truth was, James was intelligent in other forms. His creativity was out of this world, and the way he viewed the world around him was truly unique. The kid was not stupid at all, but different. David hoped that his little brother would know that as life went on.

    David also worried about Faith, and he wondered how long she could keep her composure underneath the weight of their mother's tyranny. She was such a calm spirit that he didn't want to see destroyed. She was smart and he had some confidence in her one day seeing through everything regarding Evelyn. But he didn't want to picture a version of his sister that grew cold. She had already been through enough not knowing her real parents. He truly felt for her in this aspect. She was meant to be better off with this family, but she wasn't.

    These wounds cut deep. So deep. David knew how much he hurt inside. The fear could eat him alive if he gave in to it. Maybe if he had a family to believe in, the concept of believing in God would be easier. How selfish was he really to leave them all alone? He really was like his father, running away from confrontation. Making life easier at the expense of the ones who loved and counted on him.

But David also wondered when what he wanted and needed was going to matter. This pattern of doubt and misery could go on forever if he didn't take control of his life. That was one of the hardest things anyone could do: take control of their lives when the people around them already had plans for them from the start.

As David drove along with his thoughts, he found himself at a stoplight. He waited for the light to turn green before carefully accelerating forward.

The next series of events happened in slow motion, but also too fast. As he drove forward, a giant black truck hit his driver's side at full force. The glass shattered into a million pieces as the sound and force exploded against his every sense. His car started to flip and roll, tossing him around the car, held in only by his seatbelt, and then everything went black...

David woke up in a way that felt very similar to waking up this morning. Everything was blurry, his mind didn't pick up his surroundings right away, and he could only hear a ringing in his ears.

As the previous events began to fall into sequence, he realized he was laying on the road. Everything hurt all over. He tried to move, to roll, but he could not. In shock, David looked down and realized his legs were broken. He was able to see an ambulance and a bunch of people in uniform rushing around to help him. He was getting dizzier and dizzier, and in the descending fog, he understood he was bleeding out, fading to black once again.

He didn't know what made him do it, but he had no idea if he would live through these next moments. So, he remembered his conversation with Michael and silently accepted the "real Jesus" into his heart.

His prayer was very similar to a doctor putting you to sleep. "Try your best to count to ten. 1, 2, 3, 4, 5, 6, 7......."

One moment he was bleeding, the next moment he was praying, the next moment… Nothing…

Chapter 8
The Reflection Room

David woke up a bit quicker than he normally would.

He looked around and was able to tell that he was in a hospital room. It was very quiet and peaceful, a room of all white. He tried to lean forward, but the pain in his body caused him to immediately lay back down. When he looked at the foot of the bed, he saw his legs were in casts. There was a heavy wrap around his head, a bandage to protect his head that had split open when he hit the road.

Laying his head back down he thought: "Wheelchair life is going to really suck."

He knew he wasn't paralyzed, but he knew his legs were broken. But he took a breath of fresh air and found himself grateful to be alive.

The next thing he noticed was that he was hooked up to a machine and an IV was taped to his arm. It was most likely shooting pain medicine directly into his bloodstream.

He couldn't shake the feeling of God keeping him alive. He hadn't forgotten the moment he placed his life into Jesus's hands as he bled out into the road. At that moment, it really seemed like he was going to die. It even surprised David how naturally he found himself at the feet of Jesus.

David remembered scripture mentioning how the Love of God would surpass his intellect. He remembered the scripture that encouraged him not to lean on his own understanding, but on God's.

With a moment like that, he didn't want to overcomplicate it. Michael was right, it was him that was complicating things.

Had he grown up in a house that truly followed Christ, his attitude towards it would have been different. Who knows what a good youth group could have done? What if he had more friends like Michael, or had conversations like this with him earlier in their friendship? David had hated God, he truly did. But like Michael asked, "How can you hate someone who doesn't exist to you?"

David couldn't help but think that what had happened changed everything in him. How should he feel about his mother and father now? Does he need to be a light in the Singleton house, or does he need to break away and grow with God on his own?

David knew growing closer to Jesus would be very difficult in a house like his. What was this new relationship with Jesus going to do to him as a person? He literally lived a lie his entire life. He spent his days pretending, just knowing what to say and do to pass. But this time, there would be no pretending. He really felt this, and his perspective on Jesus was not the one Evelyn pushed on them.

He knew he needed to re-read the Bible. He had only read it because he had to, and he read the book with hate in his heart. It didn't matter if it held wisdom, he hated God. But now, he wanted to read the Bible through new eyes. He felt excitement in his heart, and he couldn't wait to piece together the greatness of God. He knew that he couldn't truly save anyone unless he knew what he was reading first. He knew enough to know that Evelyn never had it right, but he needed to piece together how to explain what a walk with Jesus really was. He assumed he would be spending some time in this bed, so maybe this could be his reflection room.

Honestly, he looked forward to a guilt-free life. One where it was okay to fall short of things. He understood he wasn't meant to use grace as an excuse to never grow, but he was able to use it as a savior for his bad moments. A huge weight was lifted off of his shoulders. He was leaving a fearful relationship and entering into a loving one. Anything he gave up in his life would be through love for Jesus. Any area in his life that showed growth would be through thankfulness. He was going to read the Bible for the right reasons for the first time in his life. He truly wanted to get to know the God behind the pages.

He couldn't wait to tell his siblings the truth. They didn't have to cry for every mistake. They didn't have to hate themselves for every sin. But they could cry for the right reasons and love themselves because they were God's. He knew the idea of being made in the image of God. Evelyn used this to force perfection on them. Now saw this as a way to view himself. How could he hate himself? He was made in the best image he could possibly be made in. He was already reflecting on his infinite worth. He just couldn't wait to tell his brother and sisters.

  He wondered why God didn't take him away in the accident. What was he supposed to do on Earth? Was he on a mission? WAS there more to be learned? He had no idea why his life was spared. He felt complete peace about going to Heaven when the moment presented itself. But he felt peace about waking up, as well.

  While he was anxious to live this new life, he was also excited to see himself be the best version of himself that he could be. He actually hoped, no, prayed that he could get into Liberty University now. He could be around other Christians and learn this walk better there than he could at home or on his own.

  He knew God was real because he felt so much joy in his heart.

This was absolutely crazy! He was in a hospital bed, hooked up to a machine, bandage around his head, with two broken legs! But he was so happy, and it was all because of this new hope he found. It felt like a door had been locked in his mind, but he finally found the key to unlock it. This led him into the largest room in his mind, this place once sealed off and unknown. He felt like he had lived with a veil over his eyes, but it was finally lifted and he could see a new world.

Life seemed a lot more exciting to him. It seemed limitless and full of purpose. And he couldn't wait to step into it.

The peaceful silence was interrupted when the door opened. A female nurse walked in and Faith walked in after. Faith burst into tears and ran ahead of the nurse and hugged him tightly.

"Oh my God! Oh my God! You're okay David!" she cried.

"Yes, I'm okay," he replied happily, as he held her close.

The nurse walked towards the machine and seemed to be checking the status of it. She made her way towards him and told him how lucky he was to be alive. "You were hit by a drunk driver. He, unfortunately, didn't make it," said the nurse.

David couldn't help but feel anything short of compassion for whoever hit him. He felt sad about it, not angry. He was alive after all.

He wondered what kind of person the drunk driver was. If he was a man of sorrows, it was a shame he had to die unhappy. It was unfortunate when temporary pain led to permanent death. Sometimes people lead from out of hurt and not logic. The drunk driver could have been a man who just lost his wife and kids. Maybe his best friend passed away and he couldn't cope with it. Maybe he couldn't find the purpose of his existence, so he spent his days at the bar. Maybe he was just out having a good time, and that single moment led to his death. David felt terrible thinking that sometimes a moment of weakness could lead to the end of it all.

"Mama, James, and Ruth are downstairs in the cafeteria. Everybody is very anxious to see you!" said Faith.

David was actually pretty worried about seeing them because the last time he saw them it was a disaster. He nervously looked at his sister and asked if they were still angry with him.

"Any anger towards you went away quickly. The moment they heard you had gotten into an accident," said Faith. She seemed so angelic to him, peacefully holding his hands and resting her head on his chest.

"I was so selfish to leave you guys behind," said David as he ran his fingers through her hair.

She looked back up towards him and said, "I am the sibling who is actually on your side. I am smart enough to know that Mom isn't right. She scares me, David."

He rested in silence at that revelation, trying to find the words he wanted to reply with. He didn't want his sister to ever feel the things he felt growing up with Evelyn. But here she was, faced with the same harsh reality that he dealt with his entire life. It was only a matter of time before the others caught onto the things that Faith had. They were all smart kids, so it wouldn't surprise him if they all feared living with Evelyn eventually.

He wanted Faith to smile again, to feel happy about something in the midst of everything that had happened, so he avoided talking about Evelyn and decided to share his encounter with her. "Well, I want to tell you something... I accepted Jesus into my heart. I really did. I know you have no reason to believe me, but it is real this time."

Faith's eyes began to water and she smiled so big that she actually showed her teeth. "I believe you, God bless you."

"Faith, I don't want you to jump right into this with Mom and the others. But, I wanted to tell you while you were here. Jesus is not who you think he is. He is far better. There is more love, more grace, more mercy in him, and you don't have to live the way you have been. I really want you to read the Bible and not be afraid to see what you see. Just because Mom says something, it does not make it true. We will have plenty of moments to walk through this together, but he is real to me. He will become real to you when you see him the way you truly see him."

Faith couldn't stop smiling, and she tearfully shook her head yes, planting a kiss on David's forehead.

"So what is Mom saying about me?" David asked nervously.

"She was really upset, she started banging her head on the wall when you left. Between us, I said it once and I will say it again, even I am starting to think she's getting a little out of hand. I don't know what James thinks, but Ruth is all about Mama. But the second Mama received the call, she picked us up from school and sped to the hospital. She was really worried on the way and was very grateful to hear that you were going to be okay. We all prayed over you while you were asleep."

David smiled and told his sister that he was happy to hear everyone wasn't hateful towards him.

The door opened and Evelyn walked in with James and Ruth. Just like Faith, they all cried and embraced him. It was like deja vu hearing the same things over again. "You're okay! You're alive! Oh my God! We prayed so hard!" James remained quiet and shy, but even he couldn't stop smiling.

Ruth was extremely energetic and apologized for everything she said to him. "I just couldn't live with myself if that was my last conversation with you. I love you so much no matter what you believe," said Ruth tearfully.

David smiled back and said, "Well, if you prayed for me at all, it worked. I had a moment where I thought I wasn't going to make it and I actually accepted Jesus into my heart." It felt like the big 'surprise!' at a birthday party. Everybody except Faith and the nurse started to leap for joy.

Evelyn made her way to the bed and held David very tightly. She began to weep uncontrollably and told her son how thankful she was that he was okay. "You don't have to leave the house, we can work through this. I am so happy you found Jesus, we did pray." she cried.

"It's okay, Mom, we have lots to talk about and plenty of time. I honestly don't know where I am going to stay, but we are okay and that's all that matters," said David.

"You are absolutely right," replied Evelyn.

The nurse waited out the thankful celebration before she told everybody that David was going to be kept overnight for check-ups.

"How long was I out for?" asked David.

"Two days," replied the nurse.

"Wow, so I missed graduation?" said David sadly.

Evelyn gave him a look of genuine compassion and said, "I know that hurts honey, I was going to see you walk no matter what. But your diploma is with me, and we are all so proud of you."

It really warmed David's heart to know that his family had every intention of going to his graduation despite their argument. "I am just thankful to be alive."

The Singletons all hung out in the white hospital room for the next couple of hours. It felt amazing because this seemed like the first time in a long time where they were a normal family again. James was talking about the new Batman comic, Faith was excited about the new book she was reading, Ruth felt like she was growing closer to God, and Evelyn had a more descriptive and spiritual version of everything Ruth had to say.

As time went on, Evelyn told the younger siblings that she was going to drop them off and come back. This didn't really bother David. He actually hoped for a civil conversation between him and his mother.

His younger brother and sisters all said their happy goodbyes, and Evelyn smiled and said, "I will be right back."

"Can you bring me a Bible?" asked David. The answer was "Yes," of course, and they all walked out the door.

David was alone in the reflection room once again, and he took full advantage of this time. It had not been the plan for him to go straight into sharing his encounter with Jesus, but it kind of slipped out.

Alone, he said some prayers and felt peace. It was amazing to pray and actually feel like he was being heard. He believed in his heart that everything was going to be answered. It led him to wonder why people didn't pray more. If they believed there was a Heavenly Father who could do anything and give them anything, why didn't they pray more? Why not depend on him for everything? David laid back and thought about a new life where he prayed about everything.

Through prayer and reflection, he made the decision to not hide ever again. So, he was going to muster up the courage to tell his mother how he wanted to walk with Jesus. He wasn't going to be disrespectful, but he was not going to walk back on his path either. He was hopeful that he could bring her to realize the truth as well.

But as much faith as he now had, he was not a fool. Evelyn was sick, she was very set in her ways, so the chances of her changing were very slim. He wouldn't even be surprised if she had found some way to be upset with him about his encounter.

As he laid down peacefully, the white room was slowly turning dim. The time was going by quickly and the room had turned dark. He had the nurse check on him every once in a while, but the privacy was very good.

His time with Jesus felt intimate. He felt connected to God for the first time in his life. After a while in silent contemplation, the door opened and Evelyn walked in with his Bible in her hand. He couldn't believe how quickly the time was going. He had been in a full state of meditation.

She grabbed a chair and pulled it up towards his bed. As she sat in the chair, she placed his Bible on the nightstand next to the bed. "Here it is," she said casually.

"Thank you," he replied.

"I just can't express how happy I am to see you here," she said tearfully.

David remained peaceful but it was hard to speak. He felt a bit awkward like there was so much that needed to be said between the both of them. It hung unspoken in the air.

She too was able to feel the awkwardness that filled the atmosphere of the room and tried her best to smile through it. In an attempt to make the moment a happy moment, she asked David about his encounter with Jesus. There was a part of him that wanted to avoid this topic, but he knew that it was eventually going to be brought up. He wasn't even surprised at how quickly it came into the conversation.

"Mom, it was really crazy because it was a life or death moment. I was bleeding out on the road, my legs were broken, and I could just feel my life was running out. I had to place my faith in something and I placed faith in Jesus to bring me into heaven. But I woke up."

She looked like Mom again, motherly and warm with that peaceful smile. "Sometimes it takes a moment like that sweetheart. I am happy you saw the light, and I am happy to have you here. But more importantly, I couldn't find peace in the fact your last moments would be turning on me." said Evelyn sadly.

David felt a bit nervous and knew that it was not going to be an easy conversation. But he was not going back to who he was. He was not willing to backtrack no matter what. Life was way too short to live it in constant fear. Fear of how one would take his opinions, fear of who he is causing a confrontation with, and fear of him being in the same room as his mother.

He took a chance and just went for it. "Mom, look, I am sorry if I hurt you. I never want to hurt you. But I did not betray you."

Evelyn's peaceful look was transforming into an angry grin and she replied, "David, I couldn't believe the things you were saying to me, you are supposed to honor me as your mother, then to leave like that, you did betray me."

He just couldn't believe it, even in a hospital bed, she could not accept being wrong. It didn't even take her five minutes to stir up confrontation. He sighed and progressed forward into the conversation. While being aware of his tone, keeping it in check, he began to speak to his mother. "Mom, what you did was wrong. You hurt James. I just can't let you pull on his hair and make him feel the way you made him feel that morning. I know you want to have faith and believe that God made him wise beyond us but… He does have a learning disability, he doesn't comprehend things as easily as we do. You were making him feel stupid, and you hurt him."

She was now looking irritated. She also took a deep breath and began to reply, "I doubt the faith you claim to have. I know he is capable of greatness."

"I never said he couldn't be capable of greatness," interrupted David.

"Let me speak," snapped Evelyn. David said sorry and told his mom to continue. "I think he is living in his own world, he doesn't care about academics. I don't believe what teachers are trying to tell me, I don't think anything is wrong with him. I claimed wisdom over his life and he is choosing to be average. That is sin and he needs to see repercussions for that choice."

"Okay mom, so even if he is super smart, but doesn't push himself for perfect grades, you can't hurt him," said David.

"Who are you to tell me what I can and can't do as a mother?" snapped Evelyn. She was shaking uncontrollably and seemed very worked up. She glared at him and said, "you have no idea what hurt is and neither does James. My Mom made sure I knew what hurt was!"

The room was now silent and she didn't look like she said all she wanted to say. She wiped the tears off with her arm and said, "David, what God did you see? He hates sin, he wiped the world out with a flood to start over. He burned Sodom and Gomorrah to the ground. All because of his hatred for sin!"

"He also sent Jesus to die for our sins," he replied.

"So, he hates sin so much he sent his only son to die for it," said Evelyn.

"Mom, he died for sin to leave room for our imperfections. We can't do this on our own. It's impossible."

Evelyn was looking angrier than ever but knew she had to keep her voice down in a hospital. With a quiet but snappy tone of voice, she started to talk. " This is not God, David. This is deception. The enemy made sure to whisper these lies into your ear before you passed out. God demands our best, and we need to be perfect like he is perfect. He hates our sinful nature and we deserve punishment when we do wrong."

"Mom, do you really think God wants you to cut yourself? To burn yourself, to hit your head against the wall, to hurt us? Do you really believe that's what he wants?"

Evelyn, with her angry facial expression, replied, "He wants us to not be sinful. He wants us to be Holy! Without blemish. The punishment is necessary because it will push us to worship him the way he deserves to be worshipped."

"Well, I worship because I want to, not because I have to," said David.

"That's because you are believing lies. You are deceived by the enemy, snapped Evelyn in angry retort.

"Why do you always have to be right? You never consider what anyone else has to say," said David.

"I am right because He speaks to me," replied Evelyn.

"Well I feel like he's speaking to me," said David.

She laughed sarcastically and rolled her eyes, "You hear a voice, but it's not the Lord's voice. You are being deceived because you can't discern the difference between the two. You are on a path to wickedness and I pray you find your way to the one true God."

David shrugged his shoulders and said, "Well, I guess we have to agree to disagree. I won't do this the way you want me to do this. I'm sorry to let you down."

Evelyn's anger had now become sad desperation and she tearfully said, "I guess so." "Look, David... I am going to stay with you tonight. I am your mother after all. I think you need to get some rest."

David agreed and told his mom that he loved her no matter what differences they may have. He went to sleep with sadness in his heart. He really hoped she could understand and be happy about the faith he found, but he expected nothing less than what he got from her.

It amazed him but didn't surprise him, that she wouldn't hesitate to argue even under these circumstances. That was just who she was: Evelyn always had to say something. How much did she truly feel thankful for him? But he didn't feel the fear he had felt all his life. He was very much secure in what he said, and he was proud of himself, to say the least. She was going to have to just deal with it. This is who he was and nothing was going to change.

It was a beautiful thing to find peace in his identity. David felt he didn't need to please anyone anymore, just God. He felt that Jesus was proud of him, and that was enough for him. It was the first time he could mentally cope with his mother attacking his character. Because when you find peace in who you are, everyone else is wrong when they attack you. He felt confident that he could focus on personal growth amid the criticism. He looked forward to his newfound freedom in Jesus Christ.

It was 3 a.m. and Evelyn sat in the darkroom and watched David sleep. She was in the corner silently but angrily speaking to herself. "You have my son, you have my son, you can't have my son."

Even as he slept peacefully, she glared at him from her dark corner. The only thing that could be heard was the steady beeps from the machine that followed his heart.

"You are not the Lord our God, you are an imposter, you are the deceiver," she murmured darkly.

Evelyn was quietly shaking, digging her nails into her arm. Sobbing, crying, as quietly as she could in the dark corner. But David remained asleep. He rolled around from time to time but had no nightmares. He looked as innocent as a child and as peaceful as a bird.

"You are feeding him lies, you want him to live a life of sin, you want him to burn for eternity, while you laugh at him. I will never let you take him. I know he scares you. All he is capable of, all that he can do for a kingdom that you try so hard to destroy. But I also know that you fear me, you are terrified of me. I am a warrior, my prayers are heard above many. You fear me because I am the mother of another you seek to destroy out of fear. You fear me because I have a direct line to the father. You will never have him," she whispered as she tried to catch her breath. She was shivering and silently crying all over herself. She wanted to make herself sound strong, but she felt weaker than she had ever felt. It was spiritual warfare to her, and the enemy could never know that she was weak.

As Evelyn glared at David while he slept, she continued to silently weep. She stared at him for a few more minutes until she caught a glimpse of something absolutely horrifying. His face had slowly developed into that of a demon's face, and it slowly turned its head towards her. She froze in petrified fear as the demon smiled at her. "He's mine Evelyn, he always was," it said menacingly.

She placed both hands on her mouth and her eyes opened wider than ever before.

From her dark corner in the darkroom, the demon just stared at her. After what felt like a lifetime, she quietly said, "Intimidation is a tactic of yours, and I will not be intimidated."

But the demon continued to stare at her with a big smile. A smile that contained hundreds of razor-sharp teeth. It never broke eye contact, it truly was intimidating. The evil glare of the demon left her paralyzed, the fear itself crippling.

Evelyn slowly got out of her seat and walked towards David's body. The only thing that could be heard was her silent cries and the steady beeps from the machine. She quietly pulled the pillow from under the demon's head, but it didn't stop smiling. It continued to look into her eyes and it said, "Now what are you going to do with that?"

She didn't say anything in return. She just quickly and forcefully smothered the pillow into its face and pressed as hard as she could. As she pressed hard, David's body began to shake. But with both legs in a cast and his body weak from the accident, he couldn't overpower Evelyn. She put all her body weight into it and pressed down harder.

The machine beeped from steady to rapid, and Evelyn pressed with all her might. She was silently crying but never relented with the force she used to hold down the pillow.

After a few agonizing moments of flailing fight, David's body stopped struggling and the beeps turned into a flat line.

She took a step back and saw that David's body was completely limp. She held her hands over her mouth to silence the crying and weeping. She slowly made her way to the bed and pulled the pillow from over his face. There was no demon, it was just David. But there was no life in him, he was dead.

She continued to cry and placed the pillow back under his head. She went back into her dark corner and began to cry louder and louder. "Help! Somebody help! He stopped breathing!"

The door burst open and a bunch of nurses stormed into the room to handle the situation. A couple of them held Evelyn up as her body dropped to the floor. She was crying loud and devastated.

"He just stopped breathing! He was asleep! I was asleep and I heard the machine flatline! He just stopped breathing!"

The doctor came in and tried his best to calm the scene. It was a tragedy, a nightmare. Evelyn's cries and the commotion in the hospital room penetrated the peaceful silence that once filled the reflection room...

Chapter 9
Days later

It was a few days later and Faith found herself filled with sorrow. A grief that she never imagined could ever exist within. It didn't feel real to her, it felt like a dream, a dream that she would soon wake up from. But she was wide awake, staring at her older brother David's casket...

The funeral felt lifeless as if all the life was drained from everything around her. Gravity felt heavy, the trees felt lifeless along with the sky. It felt like life was on pause. The pastor stood in front of his casket, and below him was the hole in the ground that would become her brother's new home of rest. The pastor spoke many comforting words into the microphone, but she couldn't hear a single word, only the tone of his voice.

It felt like every breath she took weighed a thousand pounds, and her eyes carried a load of tears. It was a depressing sight. Evelyn in all black, filled with grief, Faith's younger brother and sister absolutely devastated, and then a handful of family members that they never see or even talk to.

What was life going to look like without her older brother? Who could she possibly talk to about anything? David was the only one in the family who truly understood her. Who else could provide the insight and advice that he gave? There was no other David, and it had never crossed her mind to go on without him.

She couldn't help but grieve the fact that he was the best in this world. He was intelligent beyond his years, charismatic and bold, unlike her, a leader with nothing but success in his future. He had so many doors open the second he found Jesus and made his faith his own. He was going to do so much for God, and teach her so much as she grew older. But now he's gone and none of that could ever happen.

As the tears streamed steadily down her cheeks, she couldn't believe he would never be there to watch her graduate. He would never be able to see her get married or have children. She even used to ask for his help when it came to homework, and now that was over. But deep down, one of the main thoughts that stuck was, who would protect them from Evelyn?

Life at home was liveable when she had her older brother leading by example. He was the one to come into her room and check on her. If Evelyn wanted her to feel guilty for something crazy, he was the one to turn it into a joke. To her, he was the only sane one living in that house. Ruth was younger than her, James was an awkward introvert, and Evelyn was, well, Evelyn. Faith didn't have any friends at school, she only had her older brother.

What was life going to be like now?

Another thing that worried Faith about not having her brother was the fact that he could psychically protect them. He was stronger than Evelyn, practically a grown man. A tiny woman like their mother could never be capable of bringing physical harm to a man. But all who were left were three younger siblings who wouldn't stand a chance in a physical fight with their mother.

Many people approached her at the funeral, hugged her, cried in her arms as they embraced her, held her face, and spoke long heartfelt speeches to her, but she felt extremely disconnected from everything. Every word spoken to her seemed to fly right over her head. Numb was the best word for how she felt if there ever was a word to describe it.

It was no longer the pastor standing in front of the microphone; it was now other members of the extended family. What could they possibly be saying besides, "I wish I was there more?" Nobody ever came to see them, they never received calls, only cards on holidays and birthdays. They didn't even feel like family, they felt like strangers.

"Is there anybody else who would like to say any kind words?" asked the pastor.

To Faith's surprise, James slowly raised his hand and was greeted with a sympathetic nod from the pastor. As the young boy slowly made his way to the microphone, a little uncertain and nervous, he held back tears as he stared at the closed casket. He looked into the small crowd of people and soft-spoken began to talk.

"He was the coolest guy I have ever met… I know I never said much, and I know I never said enough to him… But I wanted to be just like my brother… I still do…" James stood still with tears running down his face, shivering like he wanted to speak more but couldn't. He sniffed, wiped his tears on his sleeve, and walked back to his seat. As he returned, Evelyn and Ruth held him closely and cried.

Before the pastor could even ask if anyone else wanted to say anything, Ruth had run past him and stood in front of the microphone. With eyes full of tears and a lot of passion in her tone of voice, she began to speak, "Words cannot describe the grief in my heart. I loved my brother very much and I am going to miss him. I am going to miss his cool mellow presence in our house, his unique way of saying things, and the big brother who would drop everything to take his little sister wherever she wanted to go."

She paused for what seemed like an entire minute and silently cried in front of the gathered mourners. At last, she lifted her head and said, "I was mad at him the last time I saw him in our house, so upset with him. I just hope he knows that I am not angry with him anymore. I love him and I know he is with Jesus" Ruth's silent cries turned into weeping as she held her face and ran back to her mother's arms.

The pastor sadly made his way back towards the stand and asked if anybody else wanted to say anything.

Faith felt a strong need to stand in front of everyone and speak, but she felt so numb. She couldn't find the right words for how she felt, so what hope could she give to all these people when she really felt hopeless? Everything was falling apart and life as they knew it would never be the same. If she had the words, she would say that. She looked into the crowd and saw Evelyn slowly stand and make her way towards the microphone.

Evelyn wiped the tears from her eyes and took a deep breath before she gave her speech."It sure is something, isn't it? The power of death… It can take the strongest man and bring him to his knees, it can take the smartest woman, who thinks she knows all the secrets of the universe, and show her that she truly knows nothing… It can make a brother who never speaks all of a sudden find his voice, and a mother who feels she is always right… question where she may have gone wrong… It can take your perfect little world and flip it upside down"

The moment felt tense as everybody attending the funeral was completely silent. The gathering was all in tune with everything Evelyn was saying, but there was also a nervous look on everyone's face.

"Death also can compel a handful of beautiful people in a family to actually show their face for once. See, when I stare into this tiny crowd of so-called family members… I just can't find anyone that I recognize. Who are you people exactly? Where were you on my son's birthdays? When have any of you called our house phone? Just to see if we were doing okay? Were you going to show up at his graduation? I honestly doubt that…"

The pastor attempted to interject but Evelyn snapped at him, "This is my son! I am grieving his loss and you are going to let me speak freely!"

He immediately stepped away and allowed her to proceed. While some maintained that look of nervousness on their faces, some had pure anger struck across theirs.

"Now, before I was rudely interrupted by this wonderful man of God who never even met my boy… Since nobody here even knows us or even showed any interest in knowing us… It must have been the power of death that brought all of you lovely strangers together. All your hugs, all your kind words, all the tears I collected from you, cover my black dress... Oh, how many empty promises I have heard from you people today? 'I am here for you, if you need anything, I am always here for you.' Liars! I know the cycle! The way things work. You will call for a few weeks, maybe a couple of months, but then you will go on with your precious lives. You will forget us like you have all this time." She started to weep all over herself and was breathing faster and heavier.

The crowd was surprisingly still all ears, as nervous and angry as they may have appeared. She gradually composed herself and continued to speak into the microphone. "But feel no shame, strangers! Because as much power as you all feel death has over us... It has no power over Jesus! You see, death could not hold him down! Death was only the beginning of Christ. Death, where is your sting?" laughed Evelyn.

At this moment, someone in the crowd nervously asked her what she was getting at. Evelyn tearfully replied, "I don't know... Perhaps I am just a grieving mother who lost her baby boy..."

Evelyn slowly made her way back to her seat, and it appeared like nobody had anything to say back to her. Nobody looked at her or tried to comfort her.

It was probably for the best at a time like this. The pastor wrapped up the service and it was time to place David's casket in the ground.

As the casket was lowered into the ground, Faith couldn't stop weeping. As she cried harder than she ever cried before, her brother and sister held onto her for both comfort and strength, each one giving what they could to the others. Evelyn was weeping just as hard as her and was also holding onto her. Faith felt the reality of the moment as the casket finally made its way into the hole in the ground. From now on, she would have to speak to his grave if she wanted to speak to him at all. Just like God, she would get no response.

There were no more words spoken between the distant family and the Singleton family. They dropped flowers on his casket and quietly walked towards their cars. Even as Faith walked towards their car, she noticed nobody said a word. The only thing that could be heard on the car ride home was the silent weeping and the heavy breathing. Everybody was at an utter loss for words.

As they pulled into the Singleton driveway, Faith understood that they were in for a very long summer without their older brother.

The Singleton house was lifeless during its time of grieving. No one said much and cries could be heard behind the walls at all hours. Not only from within the walls of Evelyn's bedroom but the walls outside of everyone's bedroom.

James woke up early like he still had to get up for school. He laid in his bed and tried his best to fall back asleep, but it was close to impossible to fall asleep. His heart beat out of his chest. He could barely catch his breath. He felt like he had so much to say, but the words would never find their way out of his mouth. His mind felt overloaded with information and emotions, and he wanted to think, but he couldn't. He kept thinking to himself that if he could just take time to think about this, everything could finally come back together. But his brain was numb, and he was tired of everything.

The pain hurt so bad-- he never imagined himself feeling pain this excruciating. Death was permanent and this meant that someone he loved was never going to come back. He felt very numb and overall incapable of expressing himself.

James didn't realize it until he lost David, a person so valuable to him, that he had taken for granted having a brother who cared to understand him. The truth was that nobody ever wanted to understand him. To be honest, he didn't even know if he was weird to the other kids. He imagined he was because if he wasn't, maybe someone would have taken the time to speak to him. But nobody cared to pay him any mind. The world was just too busy for him.

He felt like there was a lot about him that could generate interest amongst his peers. There was no way that he was the only kid his age who loved superheroes. He assumed that this was a pretty common interest within his age group. As a matter of fact, this was a common interest with adults, as well.

He felt himself awakening further as he traveled within his thoughts. So he sat up, pulled himself out of bed, and began his day. The house was quiet, so he was able to tell that the rest of his family was still asleep. He was in the mood to clear his mind with a walk around the neighborhood, so he threw on some jeans and a t-shirt, and then left his bedroom.

The house felt dead to him as he stepped foot into the living room. It felt empty. There was no longer an older brother who would happily greet him early in the morning. David was gone, but everything of David's was still there scattered throughout the house, and it made things far more depressing. James never considered himself an emotional person. He felt emotionless a lot of the time. But this was absolutely heartbreaking to him.

It wasn't long before James realized he was crying silently to himself.

Collecting himself, James ate a cereal bar, then made his way out of the front door. It looked pretty outside, the sky was clear blue and everything seemed beautiful. But James felt like he would never be able to take joy in these things because he felt lifeless. Losing someone he loved was enough to take the life out of everything around him.

As he walked down his regular path, his mind picked where it left off. Yes, he had taken for granted what it was like for someone to attempt to understand him. David was the only one who took a genuine interest in knowing who he truly was. His older brother engaged him in conversation like no other ever had because he sincerely wanted to know everything that James had to tell him.

David wanted to know about the intricate storylines of all of his comic books. He wanted to understand the superpowers of every hero and villain. He would ask James questions like, 'what character do you see yourself as and why?' For every answer given, David seemed to have three more questions. David was easy to talk to because he wanted to engage people. He met them where they were and got people to talk.

Nobody ever did this at school with James. He was a ghost in the hallways; he ate his lunch all alone. James never had a close friend before, and nobody ever tried to strike up a conversation with him. James didn't really care too much about it either because he knew that he could be emotionless at times. But he truly felt so many emotions about losing his older brother. It was a beautiful thing for someone else to seek understanding in you. To know someone doesn't want anything from you but you yourself.

He found himself once again cutting through the woods and heading in the direction of Sarah's house. He wasn't heading this way to watch her. He had no intention of even running into her. It was the act of walking itself that brought him comfort. The depression filling him to the brim needed to find its way out of him, and this was his release. There was something magical about walking. He didn't have to live in reality when he walked, it was quiet and isolated from the problems that life brought him.

One day everyone would grow up: his siblings, his classmates, the children he saw playing around his neighborhood. They would grow up and want to do independent things like drive a car, but James didn't feel a need for a car because he loved walking too much. A vehicle seemed rushed with everything passing by too quickly to ponder it. It was difficult to live in a moment when it was passing by so fast. He didn't focus on the things that the average person focused on, either. It wasn't obvious like trees, street signs, addresses, interstates, or exit numbers. He was different.

Humanity was on his mind. The concepts of love and hate had found their way into his mind. Visualization kept his head in the clouds as he viewed himself in light of all he wanted to become. The questions of life and the potential answers to those questions had him occupied. It was exactly what he needed to disconnect himself from the sorrow that filled his heart.

As James followed the path he began to hear the sound of someone's voice in the distance. It was the voice of someone sweet, gentle, angelic, and soft-spoken. He felt drawn to it, so he kept walking forward. But for all its sweetness, it was also the voice of someone sad and broken. He could tell she was crying.

He casually approached the tree trunk in front of Sarah's house and, to no surprise, found her sitting on it. She was the girl he heard sobbing in the distance. Her face was covered in makeup smeared by the tears that fell down her face, and her body appeared to be limp even as she sat up. He would have been terrified with this encounter on any other day, but he felt too much already to feel anything else. James made eye contact with her and then turned to walk in the direction he came from.

"Where are you going?"

James stopped dead in his tracks at the sound of Sarah's voice. He slowly turned around and said, "I'm sorry, just walking my path. You look like you're going through it, so I'm going to leave you alone."

Sarah wiped the tears off of her face and cracked a smile at James. "I totally saw you watching me that day," she chuckled.

When he heard this, his heart skipped a beat and he froze up. "I'm sorry," he said and he turned back around so that she once again could only see his back.

Sarah got up quickly and called for him to come back. He nervously turned back around and walked towards the tree trunk.

"Can you just sit next to me for a few minutes, please? I actually am having a hard day and I could really use a friend," she asked him tentatively.

He didn't feel as nervous as he did a second ago either, so he nodded. The soft and sweet tone of her voice was soothing and brought comfort to him. James awkwardly sat next to her on the tree trunk, staring at the ground because he felt too nervous to look anywhere else. Nothing was spoken between them those first few moments. James looked for something elaborate or significant to say, but he couldn't find the words. "What's wrong?" he finally asked, apprehensive.

"It's my older brother, I just miss him," replied Sarah. The mood felt mellow and peaceful, and he could tell that he was finally going to learn something about the beautiful high school girl that he liked to watch from a distance.

"I'm listening," said James quietly.

"He's a basket case. Drugs, alcohol, in and out of jail. He is always in something. And then you have me, the complete opposite. I do everything right. Good grades, clean life, no trouble making friends, hard worker, a better person overall. Yet, my mom always favored him. She always had an excuse for him, always bailed him out of everything, she seriously babied him his entire life."

James was dumbfounded. He related to one thing: that he missed his brother, too. But, unlike her brother, David was perfect. He snapped out of his thoughts and saw that Sarah was staring at him as if she wanted him to say something. He quietly cleared his throat and told her that he was still listening.

"But me and him were always close. We talked about everything and he was the one showing me all this awesome music I listen to. I never let him know about my resentment towards him for being the favorite. I just played the role of the good sister."

"Was he always like this?" asked James out of genuine curiosity.

Sarah appeared to be gathering her thoughts, he could tell she was a thinker. It was obvious by her cycle of speaking and pausing, speaking and pausing. "For the most part, but you are who you hang out with," said Sarah. "I miss him so much. He's doing a year sentence for selling drugs. I'm here because me and my mom just got into a pretty bad fight. I told her that he was always her favorite. That my voice had never been heard. I told her that I was everything she could want in a child and that she couldn't even appreciate it because of him. Well, she's locked herself in a bathroom crying her eyes out. The truth isn't always easy to handle."

"No, it isn't," agreed James.

The world came to a complete stop as she looked him dead in his eyes. She smiled at him like he was the only boy she ever knew. The tears sparkled in her eyes and he felt butterflies in his stomach. "It absolutely means the world to me that you listened to all my complaining," said Sarah as she wiped her eyes again.

"You didn't need an answer, you just needed someone to understand," he replied calmly.

She leaned in and embraced him tightly. As her arms wrapped around him, the butterflies in his stomach began to take off. He remembered his brother once telling him to always listen when a woman speaks. Ask them questions to affirm you are listening. Pretend to care and she will easily fall for you. He couldn't believe it was really working!

He couldn't believe this was actually happening. Sarah fell in love with him! He saw their entire life together in a second's flash. Nobody outside of his family has ever shown love towards him before. The moment seemed perfect, it felt so right. As she pulled away from the hug he leaned forward and kissed her on the lips.

She quickly jerked away, shock written into her once utterly forlorn expression, and said, "I am so sorry, kid, I don't like you like that."

James began to shake uncontrollably and tears built up behind his eyes. "I'm sorry," he said quietly as he shivered.

"No, no, no, I'm sorry. This is all my fault. I must have misled you somehow. You are so young. I'm way too old for you," said Sarah softly.

"No, you're not Sarah. You're not too old. I love you," cried James.

Tears were once again falling slowly down her cheeks as she placed her hand on his shoulder. "Honey, I just don't like you that way, but we still can be friends. You will make some lucky girl your age so happy."

But before she could get another word out, he cried and ran away.

Chapter 10
Grieving

"James Singleton is weird! A little creep!" said Kayla, out of pure disgust.

Sarah had felt terrible about leading James on in the woods, so she immediately confided in her friends Kayla, Jessica, and Kylie.

Kayla was petite and blonde with blue eyes and a stuck up attitude. Jessica was a brunette with brown eyes, and she was the one most of the guys took interest in. Kylie had black hair and was a bit bigger than her other friends. She was the quiet one out of the group. It was mainly Kayla and Jessica who had the snobby personalities.

Sarah was very different from her friends. She carried herself in humility and lived her life out of love. It didn't matter who it was, her sweet, angelic personality rubbed off on everybody who came in contact with her. She never thought that she was too good for anyone, everyone was treated with dignity. Sarah was sweet, understanding, empathetic, funny, intelligent, and loving towards people.

This was why she kept her friends close to her. She was able to love them for who they were, and they loved her because of who she was. Even Kylie felt comfortable enough to speak to her on personal levels. Sarah was often the voice of reason for Kayla and Jessica. She mellowed them out when they became too much for other people. They normally had enough respect for her to listen.

"Yeah, Kayla, I agree, the kid is super weird," snarled Jessica.

Kayla rolled her eyes and grew frustrated at the thought of James Singleton. "That disgusting little creep just stares at me when I walk home from school. He looks at me like I'm nothing but eye candy! I'm seriously afraid to even know what he's thinking about inside that tiny little brain of his. I heard he's retarded or something."

"Stop it, Kayla," said Sarah as she laughed it off. "I have met him before and he is a very sweet kid once you actually talk to him. He's shy and introverted, he's not weird. James is just misunderstood."

Before Sarah could continue building up James as a good person, Jessica interrupted her. "I heard he wears women's clothes behind closed doors. That's what my little brother tells me. He sits in class all day and draws pictures of transvestites and some other weird stuff. My brother told me he found this weird picture of a man in a dress who had killed a bunch of people. It had blood and guts all over the page!"

"Come on guys," said Sarah as she rolled her eyes again. "None of that is true, if you just talked to him for a few minutes, you would be able to tell that he is a very sweet boy. I feel terrible that he misunderstood what was happening. I broke his little heart and it honestly tears me apart to know that. I don't know why I even told you two about him trying to kiss me. Have a heart, guys."

Jessica had a sinister grin and expression on her face. She giggled and said, " He's probably a little serial killer in the making. I bet my mom that he's killing animals and burying them in the ground!" Kayla erupted into laughter alongside Jessica as Sarah remained silently dumbfounded. Kayla did what she could to calm herself down so that she could dig deeper into James Singleton.

"He has two sisters at home. You know he's constantly sneaking into their bedrooms and stealing their bras and dresses!"

"James! Stop using all my make up! It isn't cheap! Why do you have to be so weird all the time?" yelled Jessica as she imitated his sisters.

"This really isn't anything to play around with, Jessica! He could be a little Jeffrey Dahmer or something. That guy was a creep. He raped guys and killed them! The guy used power drills on his victims. He wanted to make love to cold Zombie corpses. He used to pick up dead animals on the side of the road and collect them. The little creep had tiny rodent bones in his secret hideout!" yelled Kayla.

"Oh my God, Kayla! Do you think James Singleton has a baby Dahmer hideout? We should go find it!" laughed Jessica.

"Come on guys, you are both being ridiculous," said Sarah.

"I still think it could be worth searching for. He probably does have a hideout. At the least, he has a hideout because he's a loser with no friends. All losers need a hideout," giggled Kayla.

Jessica and Kayla both laughed and continued to tell made up stories about James. Sarah tried to laugh it off and not make too big a deal out of it. They all hung out for a little while longer, walking around the neighborhood slowly until they decided to go their separate ways home. Kylie was nearly next-door neighbors with Sarah, so they walked in the same direction.

"Sarah, I heard from my mom that James just lost his older brother David. They just had the funeral, and I imagine he was close to his brother. I don't feel right making jokes about the kid," admitted Kylie. This news came as a complete surprise to Sarah, and it brought tears to her eyes. She felt terrible that the little boy had to deal with the feeling of rejection in addition to grieving.

Kylie stopped dead in her tracks and felt guilty that she might have spoken out of turn. She reached over and held Sarah close, apologizing for making her feel guilty.

"Stop, Kylie, I know you didn't mean to make me feel bad, I just didn't know about his brother. It makes me wish that I would have asked him how he was doing. I didn't even ask if his day was going ok. I was so wrapped up in my own little problems. I should have been more thoughtful," cried Sarah.

"I somewhat understand how that kid feels," said Kylie. "He's alone all the time and it's sad. I was like him, you know. It felt like I was a ghost in the hallways. Nobody noticed me. I wasn't cool like everybody else. I wasn't pretty, I didn't have any common interests with the other students, and I was too shy. I didn't know how to talk to anyone."

It was difficult for Sarah to hear this from Kylie, but it gave her insight to James. It was Sarah who first spoke to Kylie while the others never took notice. Sarah wondered now as she did often why it was so hard for some people to be decent. It was the simple things that could make all the difference to someone. Smiling at someone, speaking to them, listening, treating them with kindness. But even though being decent was common knowledge, nobody ever cared about it anymore.

Both Sarah and Kylie had reached a stopping point in their walk where it was time for them to split off to their separate homes. The time during which they had walked had passed by quickly, and Sarah was left with a lot to think about. It was safe to say that she was being too hard on herself, but that didn't matter. She felt terrible for what James could be feeling and wanted to fix it right away. Before Sarah turned to her own house, Kylie spoke up one more time.

"You saved my life, Sarah. I was on the verge of killing myself when I met you. My parents ignored me, the whole school ignored me, but you actually talked to me. Do you even know how much that meant to me? I wanted to do this world a favor and actually disappear. I already didn't exist. All I needed was an act of kindness. I hope you find that kid and make things right."

They both started crying again as they walked towards their homes. One girl had tears of sadness and guilt. The other girl had tears of joy because she was thankful to have been noticed by someone. Life was easier when you could live it with friends.

****

Faith was physically drained. It felt like she had not slept all week. Her mind was far too crowded to allow any kind of rest. She tried her best to sleep but it was like her body would not let her. So, every night since the funeral has been exhausting. Her eyes would be closed for what felt like an entire eight hours, yet she was wide awake the whole time. If she did manage to fall asleep, she was confronted with nightmares of her brother David in his open casket, waking up from the horrible pictures of that day embedded in her mind.

Faith had just woken up to that image of her brother lying dead in his open casket. As she quickly sat up, she realized it was still dark outside. She looked over at her alarm clock and saw it was only three in the morning. She let out a deep sigh because she knew that she was in for a long night.

The Singleton house was as quiet as a mouse, everybody else fast asleep. In that silenced and stillness, she sat still for a few minutes, holding her head in her hands in sorrow.

As heavy tears began to fall from her eyes, she was taken back to the moment she saw her brother in his casket. He was so still, cold, and cleaned up. The makeup on his face was a sad attempt to make him look like himself, but that was not her brother lying there.

Staring at his corpse, she couldn't bring herself to fully believe this was really happening. It felt like something out of a movie, and later she would be able to walk into the bright sunlight after hours of darkness in the theater. Sometimes a work of fiction could draw you in, but the sunlight reminded you that it was never real. But unlike those films, this was not going to be easy because this really was happening, and her life was changed forever.

Before she knew it, she was back in her dark bedroom weeping uncontrollably. It felt overwhelming and her tears had no end. Sometimes crying can be relieving, but not this time. The harder she cried, the more sorrow made its home in her heart. She held her mouth tightly to smother her sobs. It was hard to breathe as her entire body was wracked with cries, and she feared that she would work herself up to death. So, she laid back down, tried to calm herself, and buried her face into her blanket.

She didn't sleep that night, but her blanket was covered in wet tears by the time the sun rose with a new day.

****

James woke up early that same morning completely numb. He wiped the crust off of his eyes and immediately started playing a new video game that Evelyn had bought for him. He had been surprised when his mother randomly took him to Gamestop, mainly because it was so soon after David passed away. It was the day before the funeral to be exact. It must have been her way of cheering him up.

Of course, a video game could never take away the pain he felt, but it could take him away from reality for a while. From the many games in the store, he chose an open-world game that would take a long time to complete. Something that would consume all of his time and force him to think deeply so that he would not think about his brother, the funeral, or any of the depression that came with losing someone he loved.

It also broke his heart that he was rejected by Sarah. James was afraid to go for walks around the neighborhood like he normally would for fear that he would see her, so he stayed in his room all week playing his video game. He would wake up each morning, play his game, go to the fridge occasionally for food, play his game some more, then go to sleep. It was very easy for him to get away with smuggling all the food he wanted because Evelyn had locked herself inside her bedroom since the day of the funeral.

A new video game should feel exciting, but it didn't feel like anything special. He felt no emotional attachment to it; he wasn't even excited when he got it. Normally there was pure excitement when he played a new video game for the first time, but he was far too numb to feel anything now. He just wanted to keep his mind busy. It was too painful to think about Sarah, and it was far too painful to think about David.

****

Ruth sat on her bedroom floor with her Bible open, but she couldn't bring herself to read it. She couldn't stop crying. Whenever she would try and read a passage of scripture, her eyes would water up and the words would get blurry on the pages. Though she had a deep desire to turn to God, she didn't know how to. It was impossible to focus on anything except her brother. She even tried to pray, but she couldn't speak a single word of prayer without sobbing.

She could barely hold herself together from the grief, and she felt an enormous amount of guilt on top of the sorrow. Her last moments with her brother were when she told him to leave and never come back, and she knew that she had been a brat toward him in the weeks before that. She just wanted to be like Mama, so she jumped on his case about anything she could. She knew that he was annoyed with her for it, but he was nonetheless patient with her. He even laughed off most of her bratty moments.

She was a terrible sister.

She found herself yelling and crying harder than she had ever cried before. In a fit of grief, she took her Bible and threw it across the room. Faith must have heard the screams because she ran into Ruth's bedroom and rushed towards her. She hugged her little sister and held her as close to her as she could. Ruth found security in her older sister as she cried in her arms. As the tears began to drench Faith's t-shirt, she ran her fingers through her sister's hair and quietly sang to her.

"I was so mean to him, Faith," said Ruth as she wept. "I was not the sister I should have been to David."

As the tears came down harder and she found it nearly impossible to breathe, Faith struggled to find the right words to say. "Ruth, he loved you so much and I know for sure that you brought him joy." But Ruth just cried harder and Faith couldn't help but feel terrible for how much pain her little sister was feeling at this moment. She gently held Ruth's face and told her, "Do not buy into the lie that you were a bad sister. He loved you and you had more beautiful memories than you did bad." Ruth placed her head gently on Faith's shoulder and cried silently.

The house had a dreary feeling to it. It didn't even look the same to Faith when she wandered from room to room. It was odd seeing David's belongings around the house, knowing there was no David anymore.

A few minutes after Faith held her little sister close to her, calmed her down a bit, she got up to get some food from the kitchen. The house was dark and completely lifeless. As she made her way through the skinny hallway, she would see things that belonged to David. A beanie that he loved to wear lay on the couch in the living room where he used to watch TV, take it off, and throw it to the side.

Seeing anything of his was enough to bring fresh tears to her eyes. The more time she spent in the house, the more she realized that every step in it was a challenge in itself. She hadn't even made it to the kitchen yet but her appetite was completely gone. No longer hungry, she turned around and headed towards her room.

She had nothing to do except read a book, so she hoped her mind could drift off into another place for the moment.

Evelyn's door was closed like it has been since they came home from the funeral, and nobody had seen her since. Everyone had in their own time quietly knocked on the door to see if she was okay, and she would assure them she was alright and send them off. But nobody had seen her since she lost her oldest child.

Faith felt immense sorrow for losing her favorite person in the world, but she also felt a deep sadness for her mother. She couldn't imagine what it was like to lose a child. She knew the saying, "No parent should ever have to bury their child."

Before she retreated into her bedroom, she wanted to check on Mama at least once. So, she walked up to her door and knocked on it. Before she could get a single word out, Evelyn called out "I'm fine…" from the other side of the wooden door.

Faith knew that her mother was not in the mood to talk and she respected that. So she walked into her own room and started to read.

****

A couple of hours later, Ruth made herself a sandwich and watched TV in the living room. There was nothing else to do in the house. Even she picked up on the odd feeling in the Singleton house. It was so dark and depressing. It seemed like everybody was trying to escape the harsh reality in their own way.

She stared at the TV rather than watch it. She didn't follow the plot, she couldn't laugh at anything funny, and she couldn't be entertained. When she had first sat down on the couch, she saw David's beanie draped on the cushion, and she took a pillow and placed it on top, lying on it. The grief that filled her was too much to handle.

After a couple of hours of watching TV, she had begun to feel an overwhelming sense of boredom. The first thought that popped up in her head was to go to David's room and bother him to drive her somewhere. But, as soon as the thought entered her mind, she was immediately reminded that this could never again be an option. The tears once more flowed and she couldn't keep herself together. She grabbed David's bennie from under the pillow and held it tight to her chest as she cried her heart out.

The rest of the day drug on like this. Everyone tried their best to escape, but all were unsuccessful. A lot of tears were shed and nobody thought about anything except David. If anyone wanted to eat, they got food themselves from the kitchen. Evelyn wouldn't leave her room, so this meant she wouldn't cook. The only ones that ate that day were James and Ruth. Faith had no appetite and even felt sick at the thought of eating anything.

It was nearly two weeks since the funeral and nothing had changed. Evelyn was still not to be seen. The Singleton children grieved, suffered from a lack of sleep, felt internal depressions, lived off cereal and ham sandwiches, and spent every day of the miserable week inside of the house. Faith still wasn't eating, and this marked the third day in a row. She only drank water. She tried to eat but she couldn't stomach anything. She was beginning to feel sick, and she could tell she was losing weight, which she saw reflected in her face in the bathroom mirror when she brushed her teeth in the morning.

On this particular day, after she brushed her teeth, she knocked on Evelyn's door to see if her mother wanted breakfast. Evelyn called out that she was okay and sweetly asked Faith to leave her be.

As the big sister she was, now the oldest of them all, Faith gathered her brother and sister and made them all a bowl of cereal.

"Are you going to eat anything Faith?" asked Ruth.

"I'm not hungry. I will eat something when I am though, I promise," said Faith.

James gave a doubtful look at her and nervously said, "But you haven't eaten anything in three days."

After a long pause of awkward silence across the table, Faith told her brother that she was okay.

"I'm worried about Mama," said Ruth sadly.

"Mama is just dealing with this in her own way. She is a strong woman, she will get through this," replied Faith.

"But she has been locked inside her room for nearly Two weeks," said James.

"Yeah! I don't think that's normal. I haven't even seen her come to the kitchen for any food! I just feel like we should try and be there for her!" said Ruth with passion.

"You guys check on her everyday and she never wants to show her face," said James.

Faith didn't want her younger siblings to worry as much as she had been secretly worrying, and she felt an internal responsibility to be the older sister that they needed. It was moments like these where she wondered what David would do. What would he say? He always knew what to say. She sighed and told them, "Look, guys, I know this is really hard, but we need to be patient with Mama. We need to let her grieve the way she wants to. We all know that she is in there praying hard and reading God's word. She is probably pumping herself up to come out of this better than she ever was."

James still had his look of doubt but didn't seem to have anything to say. But Ruth finally smiled and Faith felt accomplished to bring some kind of hope to her.

As soon as Faith was back in her room, she dropped to the floor and wept. "David, I don't know what to do. You always knew what to do. You always knew what to say. I'm just not you. I can never be who you were to them," she silently cried.

She imagined this would be an insecurity that she would carry with her for the rest of her life. She would grow up and have to deal with many situations that left her speechless. She would seek advice from people but nobody would ever be her older brother. Nobody would ever think like him and give the insight he used to give. She would have many moments moving forward where she would wonder what he would do or say.

The house was really starting to get to her head. She felt like the silence was so loud. Only the cries of her sister and the clicking of James's video game controller could be heard. But Faith needed time to think. She needed space. At only fourteen, she didn't have a car to take herself away. But, she figured she could walk around the neighborhood to get some fresh air. None of them had been outside for a long time.

As strange as it was, the depression was beginning to become an addiction. It was like stepping into a patch of thick mud and being stuck. As hard as it was to feel this, in a strange way it was easy to live in this feeling. She imagined drugs worked the same way. The user probably hated everything about them, but they made a home in it. It didn't matter how much it hurts or how much they hated it, it was home. She didn't want to leave the house, she couldn't understand why. Nobody wanted to leave or tried to leave anymore. Evelyn wouldn't even leave her room!

But just like a drug addict had a million master plans to quit drugs, not a single one involved rehab or actually getting rid of the drug cold turkey. Everybody had their way of escaping reality, but none wanted to leave their house of depression and sorrow. She felt weak but knew going outside could be a step in the right direction.

Faith walked to Ruth's bedroom and asked if she wanted to walk around outside. To no surprise, she did, but James wanted to keep playing his video game.

When the sisters walked outside, the bright sun nearly blinded them. It had been nearly two weeks since they last stepped into the sunlight. The beautiful weather felt amazing and as tiny as the neighborhood may have been in reality, it looked like a universe spread out ahead of them. Not because the outside had them in any kind of awe, but because the house they had been stuck in was so small.

As Faith and Ruth walked around the neighborhood, they began to talk.

"Faith, I have a question that's been really bothering me," said Ruth.

"Ask away," replied Faith as she chuckled.

"I was thinking about how when you go to restaurants you have to wait on your waiter," said Ruth. "And….." Ruth cracked a smile and started to laugh and said, "Well, why are we not the 'waiters' if we are the ones who have to wait for our food?"

It was strange because as dumb as this question was, they both couldn't stop laughing. The laughing actually started to hurt and caused them both to cry. As wonderful as it was, it was strange because it was the first time they had heard anybody laugh this hard in a long time.

The sun was bright, and the sky above was beautiful with no clouds. The air was fresh, and kids were playing in their front yards. Everybody seemed content walking their dogs or jogging on the sidewalks. Faith realized that it felt amazing to be outside once she took it upon herself to actually step out of the house.

The sisters spent a couple of hours outside talking about everything they could think of except David. It felt good to be two sisters having quality time during times as hard as these. But, as beautiful as the world around them looked today, it was only them who saw no true life in it. Because that's what happens when someone you love loses their life. The life around you is taken away and you have to make yourself press forward. Hoping that you will once again see life when you take a look outside.

Death was a powerful force. It doesn't matter how strong someone was, or how much they grew from the lessons of life, death can bring anyone to their knees. It could suck the life out of all beautiful things, turn feeling into numbness. Death was an unstoppable Force, a crippling entity.

Life could feel like a television show consisting of favorite lead characters who make the show what it is. Sometimes the story would take unexpected turns and lead characters would leave the show. To death, leaving the plot, it doesn't matter. The show was never the same without this person.

There was so much this person, this character, had to offer. Every human being was beautiful, every character unique. The world died a little bit with every life lost because the unique qualities that someone brought to the table had been lost. Yes, Death was an unstoppable force.

Seeing the outside world for all of its beauty was a symbol of hope. The light overtook the darkness and the colors stood out. It all came together like a kaleidoscope. Sometimes it was necessary to look for the light because feelings won't always line up with the truth.

It was going to be ok…

Chapter 11
Thief

Faith woke up early in the morning to the sound of quiet knocking on her bedroom door. She slowly woke herself up and asked who it was. Still half-awake, she watched the door slowly crack open.

It was just Ruth in her pink pajamas with a sad look on her face. "There is literally nothing left to eat in this house," Ruth said.

Faith took a deep sigh and sat up. "I know Ruth. I don't know what to do for you. Mama won't leave her room. I told her last night outside of her door that we were running out," said Faith with a concerning tone. Ruth had a look of sad hopelessness over her face and quietly walked away.

It worried Faith that Evelyn wouldn't leave her room. She understood and was sympathetic towards the situation, but she also couldn't help but think that her mother needed to step up and be a mother. It has been nearly three weeks since David's death and Faith felt like she was the new mother of the household. She was the one who cooked for her siblings. She took it upon herself to find things to do for everyone. She even played video games with James so he wouldn't have to feel alone. She and Ruth went on more walks. Together, they all tried to forget their pain.

But it was impossible to forget about him. In fact, they all shared an internal fear of forgetting him. What if not thinking about him caused them to forget him altogether? It was a convincing thought. He was the best brother a sister could ask for, he deserved to be remembered. But it just wasn't healthy to dwell on it. She felt very numb, and it was difficult for her to be strong for her little brother and sister.

She slowly pulled herself out of bed and headed towards the kitchen. As she looked through the cabinets for food, she saw for herself how little food they had left. She glanced in the refrigerator with high hopes of finding anything she could for her siblings to eat. But no luck. She was worried about upsetting Evelyn but was even more worried about her siblings having nothing to eat. So, she decided she would once again make an attempt to bring her mother out into the world.

As she made her way towards Evelyn's door, she felt a strong sense of anxiety. These days, Evelyn was unpredictable. Faith didn't want to get hit, yelled at, or disrespected in any way, but it was better it be her than anyone else. When she stopped at the door, she took a deep breath and nervously knocked on it.

"I am fine," yelled Evelyn.

"Mom, I know you are, you say that every day, but I think you should come out," said Faith nervously. There was a long deafening pause before any reply was given. Confused at the lack of a reply, Faith started to speak again. "We are completely out of food. The kids are starving and we need you to come out."

"Leave me be!" yelled Evelyn aggressively.

Faith rolled her eyes and stormed down the hallway in a fit of anger. She told both of her siblings that she would be back soon. She headed towards the front door, opened it, and walked outside. She couldn't help but speed walk through her neighborhood, she was so irritated with her mother.

She hated what she had on her mind, but it seemed like the only way to get food.

She knew there was a gas station ahead of her, she had no money, so she would have to steal something.

Faith had never stolen anything in her life, and she never wanted or imagined actually doing that. As she walked down the sidewalk path that led to the gas station, she found her mind in a panic. Would this make her a bad person? Would she go to Hell for stealing? Was this going to be something she had to do every day to feed her family? Why did she even have to worry about this when she was barely a teenager?

If Evelyn would just be a responsible parent, nobody would be starving. Faith felt immense anger about that. How many more weeks or months before they see their mother again?

On the other hand, Faith didn't know if they wanted to see Evelyn. Life could be a lot more difficult dealing with her. It wasn't a good sign to not see their mother for nearly three weeks. Evelyn would probably be on edge, a ticking time bomb. She already burned herself on a stove, now she lost a child. What was going on in her head these days?

Faith felt like if David were here, he would be doing exactly what she was doing to care for her family. She didn't think he would call it the right thing to do, and she never saw him steal anything, but he took care of them just as much as their mother did. He would probably be proud of her for stepping up and taking matters into her own hands.

Still, she had deep fears of being caught, she was not a master thief, how do you even steal something?

Before Faith knew it, she was outside of the gas station. She found herself frustrated at the fact that the trip didn't go by as quickly as she wanted it to. She was in no hurry to walk into a place of business and steal anything. But that was usually how life worked: the exciting moments felt like forever away, while the bad moments occurred so quickly.

Faith was more nervous than ever as she opened the door and walked into the gas station.

When she stepped into the bright store, it immediately felt like all eyes were on her. Like everybody in the building knew what she came to do. She slowly and awkwardly walked through the gas station. When it appeared that no one was looking, she stuffed a tiny bag of beef jerky into her side pant pocket.

There it was, her first stolen item ever!

Faith then secretly and very quietly stuffed cereal bars into her pocket and kept moving. Nobody seemed to see what she was doing, so she kept filling her pockets and inside her pants.

Finally, once she was packed with food, she felt like she had gathered all she could hold onto, and it was time to get out of there as quickly as possible.

Nervously, she walked towards the front door but heard a harsh voice stop her dead in her tracks.

"Where do you think you're going?"

Faith quickly turned around as her heart skipped a beat and burst out of her chest. Of all people and all luck, it was a local cop getting his morning coffee. "Just walking home sir," said Faith softly but nervously.

He just looked irritated as ever, even rolled his eyes at her.

"Well, now I have to take you home myself because I saw what you did." He reached into her pockets and started to pull out everything she stole. As all the food fell to the ground, she felt tears streaming down her face, embarrassed and terrified.

"Is there more? I will find it!" yelled the officer. He looked over at the store clerk and said, "I am so sorry for her lack of respect, sir. I am going to take her home to her parents and see what they think of this."

The clerk gave a thumbs up to the officer and told Faith he never wanted to see her at his gas station again.

Sitting in the back of a cop car was excruciating. Faith couldn't pull her head out of her hands, and she couldn't stop crying. After she told the officer where she lived, she cried the entire five-minute drive there. She was dead, absolutely dead. Never once had she ever gotten into trouble like this. Punishment in the Singleton household was bad enough when cops were not involved. She feared the look on her mother's face more than the cop himself.

As the police car stopped outside her house, Faith's heart sank to the bottom of her chest and it became impossible to catch her breath.

The officer opened the car door for her and told her to get out of the car. Faith did as he instructed, wiping tears up as they both walked up to the front door.

He knocked on it a few times and someone finally answered. It was Ruth with a horrified look on her face.

"Hey, darling, can you get your Mama or Papa out here for me?" the officer asked.

Ruth nervously looked back up at him and said, "Sure, give me a second please." With that, she ran out of sight. Faith's heart beat faster than it ever had before, and she could still feel tears pouring out of her eyes.

They waited a few minutes, Faith in agony until Evelyn finally appeared.

Evelyn looked terrible! She had stains all over her white nightgown, which she clearly had not changed out of for days, weeks. She had bags heavy under her eyelids, so it was easy to tell that she hadn't had a lot of sleep. Her hair was messy, a tangle. And the look on her face when she saw Faith was a look of pure anger and hatred. "What's the problem officer?" grunted Evelyn.

"Is this your little girl?" asked the officer.

Evelyn, clearly irritated, rolled her eyes and said, "Of course that's my daughter. What did she do?"

The policeman looked surprised and a bit annoyed at her rude tone of voice, but he answered her question. "I caught her stealing food from the gas station close to here. She attempted to take quite a few things."

Evelyn began to shake and her fury showed all over her face. Instead of bursting with rage she sighed and said, "Well thank you, sir, I will take it from here." She glared at Faith and angrily said, "Get in here now."

Faith, obedient and quiet, did exactly as commanded and waited in the living room until her mother was done talking to the officer.

In those terrible minutes full of dread and anticipation, Faith could hear Evelyn giggling with the officer, making small talk. Each second of waiting fed her fear, which grew and swelled horribly.

The talking between the two adults finally came to an end. "Well, thank you, officer, for bringing my daughter back to me. I hope she didn't give you too much trouble," said Evelyn from a distance.

The officer told Evelyn it was no problem, that he was only doing his job. As soon as the front door closed, the strong sense of fear that Faith felt had increased and she trembled with it.

Evelyn appeared like an evil witch out of a dark fairytale, a look of complete anger struck across her face. She was shaking and holding tears back. Faith would have felt disappointed for letting her mother down were she not so afraid of what was about to happen.

Evelyn looked to the hallway and saw both Ruth and James standing there. They both were speechless and terrified. She glared at them and that was all it took for the two of them to run to their rooms and shut the doors.

"Well, you did it… You got me out of my room… Are you happy now?" asked Evelyn in a hoarse tone of voice.

Faith had no idea what to say, she couldn't even find the courage to look into her mother's eyes. So she remained quiet and allowed her mother to keep talking. "I shouldn't have to worry about this. Do you know? I mean, you don't think I am hurting enough already? I just lost my baby boy. He's gone, baby girl. I can't have any more moments with him. Every morning, I wait for his door to open, but then I am reminded that he isn't coming out. I can't handle it. I am really struggling."

Faith still couldn't bring herself to speak up or even look away from the floor. Evelyn was slowly pacing the living room back and forth. She was shaking and laughing quietly to herself. Laughing slightly sadistically.

"So, you have nothing to say for yourself? Really? Nothing? Nothing at all..." asked Evelyn harshly.

Faith still remained as silent as a mouse and her eyes stayed locked on the floor. This brought even more frustration to Evelyn because she marched towards Faith and grabbed her by the mouth. She squeezed hard at the cheeks, fingers digging in painfully, and made it difficult for Faith to breathe. With the frail girl now in her grasp, she jerked Faith's face upward so that the child would make eye contact with her. Faith began crying and sobbing, but her mother's hand had a tight grip over her mouth. Her cries were muffled and seemed to have no effect on her mother.

"Look at me! I want you to stop your crying and tell me why any daughter of mine is out there stealing! Tell me! Now!" yelled Evelyn. She roughly released her fingers from Faith's mouth and watched her daughter wipe her tears away.

Once Faith did what she could to compose herself, she took a deep sobbing breath and answered her mother's question. "There was no food in the house, Mama. We are completely out of food. We tried to tell you, but you wouldn't leave your room."

A look of disbelief took over her mother's face and she rolled her eyes. She sarcastically laughed and said, "So it's my fault you're stealing from people?"

Faith was terrified and felt trapped in her words. She quickly told her mother no, it wasn't her mother's fault at all. She insisted that she had made a huge mistake and would never do it again.

Evelyn once again paced the living room back and forth. She started to silently weep to herself the way Faith did. She turned towards Faith and told her to stay where she was.

Faith nodded a 'yes' toward her mother and watched Evelyn storm down the hallway. A door quickly opened, "You, come here, living room!" Then another door was violently opened, "You, living room. Right now!"

Within the next few seconds, Evelyn was back in the living room and James and Ruth were following behind her.

"I want the three of you to sit at the dinner table right now," said Evelyn quietly but angrily. So, they all wasted no time finding a seat at the table.

Evelyn followed them into the kitchen and grabbed a giant kitchen knife from one of the drawers. She returned to the kitchen table and looks of pure terror were stamped on the faces of her children.

"What are you doing, Mama?" cried Faith.

"Shut up! You don't get to speak!" screamed Evelyn.

Faith immediately shut her mouth and nobody looked away from the table.

Evelyn silently laughed to herself and began to walk in slow circles around the table. As she paced, she began to speak.

"Sin is a disease... Oh, it sure is... It is like a piece of yeast on bread. Once it infects one slice, it will spread through the rest of it. Once sin is introduced to one part of your body, then you can expect it to make its way into the rest of it. Because of sin, we have Hellfire and damnation. We have the enemy that roams the Earth like a lion, looking for a weak soul like yourselves to devour."

The moment was very tense and tears filled the eyes of everyone at the table. The silence was deafening and it felt like anything terrible could happen at any minute.

Faith was so afraid and in tune with what her mother was saying that she didn't realize Evelyn had come to stand behind her, no longer circling the children. All kinds of horrifying thoughts were filling Faith's head. Was she about to get stabbed to death? Was she going to get hit in front of her brother and sister? What was about to happen? She closed her eyes and recited a protective prayer in her mind.

Evelyn looked ahead of Faith and overlooked the entire dinner table as she continued to speak. "Ruth, baby... James... I want you both to learn from your older sister today. Okay?..." With only the sound of soft cries in the room, she grabbed onto Faith's chair and forcefully but slowly turned it around so she could face her daughter. "Look at me sweetie," said Evelyn softly.

Faith slowly wiped her eyes and looked up like her mother asked her to do. "So you're hungry? Is that it? You are hungry and you felt the need to steal from someone?" asked Evelyn.

Faith looked at her mother nervously and said, "I was getting food for James and Ruth, Mama. I'm not hungry. I haven't eaten." It was as she defended herself that Faith noticed the giant kitchen knife on her lap and Evelyn only a couple of inches away from her face. No personal space at all.

Evelyn rolled her eyes and asked Faith why she hadn't eaten as if she was very annoyed to hear this.

"Mama, I haven't been able to since David passed. I can't stomach it. I really try to eat but it makes me sick. I have lost a lot of weight, but I promise I have tried to eat. Look, you wouldn't leave your room, Mama! Ruth and James are hungry! I am sorry for stealing! But what else was I supposed to do?" yelled Faith.

Evelyn laughed sadistically and made her way towards the kitchen. Faith turned her chair back around and held her head at the dinner table. She was able to hear Evelyn from a distance. "I understand that I failed as a mother in certain areas of motherhood, but now I fail to feed you? Wow! Well, I apologize. How wrong of me sweetheart!" hissed Evelyn sarcastically.

Out of nowhere, a loud thump struck the dinner table as the kitchen knife was jammed into it. The knife was stuck right next to Faith, and she nearly jumped out of her seat from the loud impact. Before she could collect herself, another loud thump was heard as a giant bottle of ketchup was slammed onto the table along with a bottle of bright yellow mustard.

Evelyn looked across the table and calmly said, "I guess I need to swallow my pride, take some parental ownership, and step up as a real mother should! I have to make sure that my baby eats something!"

Before anyone could respond Evelyn violently grabbed Faith by her hair and jerked her head back. Faith started to cry from both fear and pain, and Evelyn opened the bottle of ketchup. Tipping the bottle and squeezing hard, Mama began to force-feed it down her throat. As ketchup poured all over Faith's face and down her throat, both Ruth and James were crying for Mama to stop.

But Evelyn ignored the cries and threw the ketchup bottle at the kitchen wall. Faith spit out ketchup, crying loudly, gagging. "Oh, I don't think you're full yet, baby! You haven't eaten in days! Here take some of this, too!" yelled Evelyn as she grabbed the bottle of mustard.

Before Faith could process a single word her head was jerked back again and her mouth flooded with mustard, filling so fast that it dribbled from her mouth down her neck, thick droplets falling to the floor with fat smacks. It burned. As Evelyn poured mustard down Faith's throat, Ruth and James screamed for her to stop.

Faith jerked her head away quickly when she could and vomited all over herself. Evelyn stepped away in time before it could get on her. "Shut up! Shut up! Shut up! Now! All of you!" screamed Evelyn. Faith kept crying but Ruth and James quit speaking at once. "You don't steal!" Evelyn bellowed.

"Okay, okay!" cried both Ruth and James almost in unison.

As Faith was still a mess and still crying, Evelyn forcefully grabbed her wrist and stretched her arm out on the table. The dramatic crying picked up again from everyone as Evelyn grabbed the giant kitchen knife and held it high above her head. "Jesus said if your eye causes you to sin, cut it out! If any part of you produces sin, then cut it off! So maybe since you like to steal, I should cut off your hand!" screamed Evelyn.

Faith was now crying harder and louder than she ever had. Humiliated in ketchup, mustard, and vomit, and now terrified that she was about to be stabbed. She just kept crying, "Please Mama! Please! Please! Please! Mama! Please! No!" James and Ruth begged their mother to put the knife down and let go of their sister.

"This will take care of the problem once and for all!" screamed Evelyn. She ignored the dramatic cries of all her children and began to count down from ten. "Ten. Nine… Eight… Seven… Six. Five… Four… Three… Two… One…"

Crack!

As the loud cries from everyone at the table filled the room, Faith looked out from a slit in her closed eyes and saw the knife had been jammed into the table next to her hand. The crying slowly turned into quiet sobbing once everyone realized that Faith still had her hand.

Evelyn looked at her children intensely and calmly and said, "You do not steal. Do you understand me?..." They each nodded yes and wiped the tears from their eyes. Evelyn frowned and said,

"Good. Now, I am going to go back to my room and spend a little more time grieving the loss of my son. I will get groceries first thing tomorrow. Is that okay?"

They all once again nodded yes, and Mama walked back into her bedroom and locked the door.

As soon as she was gone, Faith dropped to the kitchen floor and began to quietly cry. Both Ruth and James came to comfort her and helped her up. "Let's go get you some new clothes," said Ruth softly.

Faith sadly nodded 'yes' and told them both she loved them. As they all made their way down the hallway toward their bedrooms, they each heard something quite disturbing. Evelyn was loudly singing praises to Jesus behind her bedroom doors.

James went into his room and did what he always did, buried everything into his video games. But Ruth followed Faith into her bedroom and helped her find some new clothes. As they each gathered pajama shirts and pants, Faith told Ruth, "We need to get out of here."

Ruth had a confused look on her face when she heard this. She looked back at Faith and said, "Mama loves us, Faith, we can't leave her. What would we do without her?"

Faith was amazed at how loyal Ruth was to Evelyn even after everything that had happened. At this moment, she knew it would take a lot for Ruth to ever leave their mother. She looked back at Ruth and said, "You're right, I don't know why I said that."

Chapter 12
Secret Thoughts

The Singleton family got ready to go grocery shopping together the next morning. The next day felt less tense compared to the day before. Evelyn woke up on her own and even left her bedroom. As if the night before had not happened, she carried on with the regular morning routines that she had followed since before the death of her oldest son. It was strange to Faith that Mama was in a good mood.

Their mother didn't have the anger in her voice that she had recently, and she didn't appear intimidating either. She was reminiscent of the mother they all used to know. She was encouraging and even sweet when she told both Faith and Ruth that they looked beautiful that day. Ruth laughed off the compliment and said her hair was messy from sleeping. But Mama said she was always beautiful. Then, she told Faith that she was thankful to her for keeping everything together while she was grieving, and she asked James if he beat his video game yet.

Faith was happy to see this but it just didn't feel natural to see Mama so normal.

"Are we ready ducklings?" asked Evelyn sweetly. The three children made their way to the car and started to drive to the grocery store.

There was a sad moment during the drive as a news story cut into the music playing on the Contemporary Christian Station. The radio hosts spoke of multiple church shootings moving state to state. Virginia could easily be next. But, it wasn't healthy to jump to assumptions. As sad as it was to hear about these events, the worship wasn't going to stop.

Evelyn did what she always did while driving anywhere. She sang overtop of the worship music that she had playing through the speakers. James sat still with his hands on his lap, an uncomfortable look on his face. Ruth matched Evelyn and sang along to the music.

Faith tuned everything out and allowed her mind to drift into deep thought. She was beginning to feel odd about everything in her life. All she ever knew was life at home, living with her volatile mother. She didn't pick things apart too much because she had gotten used to life at the Singleton house. As Evelyn and Ruth sang as loudly and passionately as they could, Faith truly questioned everything about her life for what felt like the first time. Maybe it wasn't normal to be locked in a dark basement for getting a bad grade. Maybe it wasn't normal to have everything taken away on your birthday. Maybe it wasn't normal to watch your mother burn herself on a stove. Maybe it wasn't normal to have to do long Bible studies. Maybe Mama wasn't always right. Faith knew for sure what happened yesterday was not right. She missed David, she felt so vulnerable without him here.

Before she knew it, the car was parked and they were walking into the grocery store.

Evelyn was very loving towards Ruth, and she had the child excited about being able to choose the food she wanted for the house. She felt like Mama's little helper and found great joy in calculating the prices of everything they added to the shopping cart.

James remained very quiet and didn't seem to care about what they got for the house. He didn't want to be there; he much rather preferred being in his bedroom. He was the indoor kid who hated having to run errands with his family. Because when something needed to be done, Evelyn always made sure that it was done as a family. So, there was a lot of spending weekends driving from place to place: grocery store, furniture store, DMV, doctor appointments, they always had to go together.

The ride home could have fooled any outsider into believing they were one small happy family. Everybody laughed and sang, and Evelyn was still in a joyful mood. Faith went along with it, but she still felt disturbed by what happened the night before and some of the events leading up to it.

"When we get home, we need to dig into God's word," said Evelyn casually. She had a tone of gentle urgency as she mentioned them probably straying since David passed away. Nobody was against it either. With Evelyn locked in her bedroom for nearly a month, nobody did regular Bible studies. It was a grieving period. But the grieving never stopped.

Everyone still had a hole in their heart without David. It was the elephant in the room that was hard to address or even think about. He was in everything they saw. Driving past a building that he stepped foot in at some point would bring back memories. Driving past the school he went to would remind them of the high school graduation they never got to attend. Driving past the beach would rekindle moments of walking with their brother along the shoreline. David was in everything.

The family dove right into their Bibles when they got home. Faith read the book of Philippians where Paul said to be anxious about nothing and to pray for everything. He also spoke about setting his mind on only positive thinking. The words were needed and very timely. One of the most miraculous traits of God that Faith could never deny was that she always seemed to read the right scripture at just the right moment. Not remembering that this chapter was going to speak on the troubles she was currently facing, of course. She needed positive thinking in her life. She needed it for losing her brother, and now she sadly needed it for her mother.

Sometimes she wished their Dad never left, but they didn't have many memories of him. With the age gap between them and David, it was difficult to feel too much of an emotional connection to him. David was the one who truly remembered what it was like to have a man in the house. To Faith and her younger siblings, David was the man of the house. It just was what it was: there was no father, just Evelyn. Their mother hadn't been making much sense recently, but she was the parent that had been holding the family together.

It wasn't long before they each found themselves in the living room with Evelyn. The time had come for reflecting on the word of God.

"All things work together for the good of those who love God and are called according to his purpose. Romans 8:28," said Ruth, very childlike. It was good seeing her little sister happy again. She was normally a bit annoying when it came to the reflection time, but she had been so sad and broken for the month.

As Evelyn smiled on her little girl like a proud mother she didn't hesitate to add her two cents to the scripture. "This only applies to the children of Christ. The nonbelievers in this world don't have anything good ahead of them. They don't have hope in their lives. Not a single drop of hope. For us, everything good and bad is going to come together for our good. But for them, everything is going to fall apart. They have nothing to look forward to," said Evelyn in an uptight sort of manner.

Ruth smiled and said, "I guess that makes us the special ones."

Evelyn smiled back and gave her a nod of approval with her kind eyes. Faith wanted to mention the importance of bringing hope to the hopeless, but why bother? It was hard to tell if anything she said could ever be correct in her mother's eyes.

"Faith, what about you, sweetheart?" asked Evelyn.

She remained calm and didn't get too enthusiastic, but she told her mother what she read.

"That is the perfect piece of scripture for you to run into sweetheart… Maybe you should've prayed harder when you were hungry," said Evelyn slickly.

The sly comment raised an eyebrow, but Faith was not trying to battle it out with her Mother today. She felt like saying, "No, maybe you should have been the answer to that prayer. Be a real Mom and actually leave the bedroom and feed your children." But then what? Be punished for defying the evil queen once more? It was strange, but Faith was beginning to feel the internal bitterness towards Evelyn that David had felt.

Evelyn was still in a joyful mood and felt extremely passionate about her teaching moments. "Kids, one thing to take away from praying instead of feeling worried... If you do not have the faith that our heavenly Father requires of us, do not be surprised when you have to face the consequences of this world. Your older sister was brought home by the police yesterday, and for what? She didn't trust in Jesus and gave into her sinful desires," said Evelyn as preachy as ever.

Faith sat still with an almost overwhelming feeling of awkwardness. "But I am sure you learned your lesson, didn't you, Faith?" said Ruth in the tone that mimicked her Mother.

"Of course," Faith replied softly.

"As tragic as the church shootings are... It is very well possible that these people weren't living the life they should have been living. False prophets being led by blind prophets. False theology is poison, just as bad as the culture outside of Christ. Maybe worse..." said Evelyn.

Nobody bothered to comment on this statement. To Faith, it was very cruel and non-empathetic to the ones who lost their lives. Ruth didn't even feel the desire to back her mother on any of it. The room just went quiet until Evelyn spoke again.

"Well, what about you, James?" she said. Evelyn genuinely seemed curious about his answer.

"I read the end of the Gospel of John, where they nailed Jesus to a cross," said James, very emotionless.

The look on Evelyn's face began to go from joyful to sad and sympathetic. Immediately, tears filled her eyes and she tearfully said, "It is beautiful what he did for us isn't it, baby?"

James still didn't have much emotion surfacing, but he told her yes, which was the answer that would get her off of him the fastest.

The reflection time ended peacefully, and it was finally time to do whatever they wanted. Evelyn spent her time cleaning the house and singing soft praises to her Lord. Faith and Ruth both went for a walk outside, and James went to his bedroom. As he sat down to play his video game, he wanted to drown out some thoughts that seemed too active in his mind.

Yes, he was crushed to lose his older brother, but James had other things on his mind that he wanted to silence. He had secrets, dark secrets. It was true that he loved video games, movies, and comic books. It was also true that he was a socially awkward pre-teen who had learned how to live in his head. But what nobody knew about him was how dark the world was inside his head.

When he read about Jesus being nailed to the cross, he always felt drawn to it. He was similar to Alex from 'A Clockwork Orange' in the sense that he got pleasure from his violent thoughts. He was the Roman soldier that drove the nails through Christ's hands. He found pleasure in the cries of his captor, and he had a strange infatuation with the blood that poured down the wooden cross. He felt a strange excitement when he imagined himself to be the one to place the crown of thorns on the head of Jesus and press down as hard as he could. The blood that poured down Christ's head was a work of art, and the piercing screams were the equivalent of a Beethoven symphony.

But James didn't have an issue with Jesus. He had no hatred toward him at all. It was not the idea of harming the Son of God that interested him, it was the idea of bringing harm to something living. He had a strange fascination with death. When the children saw puppies, his sister's first thoughts would be how cute they were and how to get Mama to bring one home. But he would have to force himself not to wonder what it looked like inside. If he cut the puppies open, what would come pouring out?

His imagination was scary, and he often felt a deep sense of guilt for his thoughts. He didn't understand how or why, but he would wonder what it would feel like to take a person's life away.

He had certain triggers for these thoughts, and the kitchen knives were one of them. He sometimes had vivid visions of stabbing his little sister as many times as he could with a kitchen knife. He wondered what her insides looked like, as well. Would the color leave her eyes as he watched her die? What did it even feel like to put a knife through someone? There was a slight rush to stab boxes or thick tree trunks, but he often imagined it felt better with an actual person. Unlike boxes, a person would bleed and scream.

These dark thoughts were overwhelming, and he didn't want them to become cravings. So, James tried his best to do whatever he could to drown out those thoughts. But it was incredibly difficult for him to put them aside. They came in faster than he could unthink them, and the feelings attached to these thoughts had been growing stronger.

The true reason behind his quiet personality was the fact that he was a deeply disturbed child. He had no one to talk to about his crazy thoughts. Who would understand this? Nobody, especially in the Singleton household.

"Mama! Mama! Mama!" The front door opened and it was so loud that both James and Evelyn left their rooms to investigate. When they reached the living room, they were amazed to find that Ruth and Faith had brought a dirty cat home with them.

"No, no, no, absolutely not!" laughed Evelyn.

"Please!" yelled both of the girls at the same time.

Evelyn couldn't stop laughing at them because they were making it funny. She finally got some words out over their pleads for a new pet and told them to take it back. "We don't need a cat, absolutely not! This is not even a conversation," chuckled Evelyn.

But they both kept pleading, and it must have been adorable to Mama because she agreed to let them keep it for the day. The deal was that they were going to take it to a shelter tomorrow morning.

"I guess you two better cherish this cat for the day, love on it all you can because she is going to a shelter tomorrow," said Evelyn very sternly. She didn't need to tell them twice, they took whatever they could get and ran into Faith's bedroom to play with their one day pet.

As Faith and Ruth cuddled the cat, James stood outside the hallway looking puzzled. Evelyn looked at him with love and sweetly asked if he was okay. He quietly nodded his head and went back to his room.

As he sat down and played his video games, he continued to be afraid of his thoughts. He felt like a freak with no clue as to why he felt so dark inside. He was practically a ghost at school, so being bullied was no reason. He loved his family, and he felt like they loved him back. He had every video game he could want. He didn't feel like an unhappy child, he was just confused. But his urges scared him.

Sometimes, when everyone was asleep and the house was completely silent, he would feel the itch. The itch to stab someone to death while they slept. The way he visualized these stabbings in his mind was extremely detailed.

In his fantasy, he would tower over one of his sister's beds and spend some time staring at them. Watching them sleep, there would be a strange arousal with the thought of disrupting their peace and silence with pain and violence. When the time came, he would place his hand over their mouth and stab as many holes in them as he could. He pictured his sister's beautiful white nightgown gushing dirty red with every stab. Feathers from their white blankets would cover the room like falling snow. Every stab was a release, something therapeutic, something exhilarating.

He absolutely terrified himself because he loved it. These thoughts felt so good to him. Instead of a young teenager discovering pornography, he was gravitating toward something much darker. But he did what he could to think these sick thoughts away because he was terrified about what they could potentially lead to someday.

All of a sudden he heard light scratching at his door and what sounded like something bumping into it. He ignored the noises at first but they kept occurring, so he finally paused his game and opened the door.

It was the new cat that his sisters brought home. It was looking up at him, meowing and rolling on the floor. The kitten was showing off and most likely saying that it wanted to be held.

James bent over and picked it up, holding it close to his chest. The tiny kitten must have liked him because it snuggled into his chest and started to purr loudly. James brought it into his dark bedroom and sat with it on his bed.

As he pet the animal, he couldn't help but admire its beauty. "It's no wonder my sisters brought you home," said James sweetly. It continued to purr and cuddle against him. He held it tight, ran his fingers through its fur, and continued to talk warmly and quietly to it.

But then his dark thoughts once again started to take over. As he pet the cat's tiny head, he felt a swelling urge to smother it. To place his hand over its mouth until it stopped breathing. He wanted to cut it open and see what its insides looked like. For some strange reason, he was developing a strong desire to bring harm to this beautiful animal.

His heart was racing and beating hard, so hard he could almost hear it. He noticed that his hand was wrapped loosely around the kitten's little neck, ready to hurt it. The thought of squeezing was pleasing to him, yet disturbing as well.

He started to slowly tighten the grip on its neck until he heard a voice. "Tiny! There you are! We thought you ran away!" yelled Ruth.

Ruth ran into his room, looking for this cat who apparently now was named Tiny. "Isn't she just absolutely adorable?" asked his little sister.

He quickly let go of Tiny's neck and passed her onto Ruth. "Oh yeah, she is very lovable, she was purring when I pet her," said James.

Ruth swayed back and forth with the kitten in her arms, holding Tiny very close to her with a big smile on her face. "We just gave her a bath and she was surprisingly very good. She didn't freak out in the sink. She's a good girl. I'm really sad we have to give her away tomorrow," said Ruth very sadly.

"Well, I am sure she will remember you for everything you did for her," said James.

"I am going to steal her from you. Me and Faith are just rearranging her room, and we want Tiny in there with us," explained Ruth.

Before James could tell her it was okay to take the cat away from his room, she was gone.

Evelyn was feeling as joyous as ever while cleaning the house. She spent a while in the living room rearranging furniture, picking up trash, and dusting off counters. She vacuumed the floor to perfection and became happier the cleaner her living room got.

When she cleaned the house, it was time spent with God. She was either in deep prayer or meditation while cleaning. It gave her peace of mind. Sometimes she would feel so joyful while cleaning that she would break out into worship. Her horrible off-pitch tone could be heard from all rooms of the house. Perhaps she felt joy because she didn't clean too often-- her room was messy after all. When something was done occasionally, it was easier not to take it for granted.

Evelyn eventually cleaned her way into the kitchen. Still in a state of happiness and euphoria, she hummed praises to God softly under her breath. She threw away trash from on the countertops, wiped them down, and also cleaned out the cabinets.

Still feeding off the feeling of turning her dirty house into something new, she rearranged the refrigerator. She was so focused on worship and only worship that no other thoughts occurred to her as she cleaned the house.

The only thing she had left at the end was the sink full of dishes. She would normally make one of her children wash them, but she couldn't shake the desire to clean things up herself. Turning on the sink water, she put dish soap on the green sponge and began to wash the plates at the top of the pile.

The house was completely peaceful and the silence was wonderful. Every once in awhile joyful giggles could be heard from her daughters who were playing with their one-day pet. James was always quiet, he either stayed in his bedroom with the door closed or he went on walks outside.

The sound of the sink water pouring over the dishes was interrupted by a familiar voice. "I bet it feels great to finally forget about me."

At the sound of his voice, Evelyn's heart nearly came to a complete stop. She was petrified as she slowly turned her head towards the familiar voice that was heard behind her.

It was David!

He stood a few inches away from her, pale as a ghost, still in his hospital gown with his hair a mess from being smothered to death. With a sinister smile on his face, he leaned on the kitchen counter. "I hope you don't mind, Mom, I'm going to sit on the counter. Believe me, you would want to sit down after laying in a dark coffin for as long as I have," said David as he happily hopped on top of the counter.

"You can't be here... You can't be real," said Evelyn as she shivered, tearful.

David laughed and said, "Oh, I'm really here, Mom. Especially for you. I just wanted to check on you."

Evelyn was frozen, all the color in her face gone, and she couldn't stop trembling. Not a single word left her lips as she looked upon the son she never expected to see again.

"Aw Mom, what's wrong? You don't look happy to see me. Don't be rude, I miss you. Here, give me a hug."

David hopped off the kitchen counter and embraced his mother. Evelyn was terrified by how real his arms felt around her. He was cold and lifeless, but clearly here in this very moment. He reeked of dead flesh; it was unreal that she could smell him at all. He held her close, and it wasn't long before she began to cry into his hospital gown. She got chills down her spine as he slowly made eye contact with her, giving her a sinister crooked smile.

She couldn't find the words or the courage to speak up. He wouldn't look away from her, but his smile suddenly turned into a sorrowful frown. "How could you send me down there, Mama? It's terrible. This is the first time in what feels like a hundred years that I've seen my skin look so... not burnt."

Evelyn's hands covered over her mouth as she continued to cry. This was the last thing she wanted to know. He was now also tearing up, his ghoulish look now turned into a presence of sorrow.

"Time is infinite where you sent me, Mama. It can be so dark, but never cold. I have been burning for years. I have burned in flames for more years than I spent on Earth. It's horrible." David was crying, having a difficult time keeping himself together. He wiped the tears out of his eyes, tried to keep himself from shaking any more than he already was, and spoke more chilling words to his mother.

"Sometimes they don't burn me, though... They cut me, too. Here, look!" said David enthusiastically as he held his arm into plain view. It was covered in hundreds of gruesome cuts so deep he looked shredded. His muscles and bone were exposed as blood poured down his arm.

Evelyn fell down to the kitchen floor, crying harder but trying to remain quiet. She did not want her kids to find her or see David.

David pulled his arm away from his mother, chuckled, and kneeled down to where she was. He whispered to her, "Hey, look at me..."

But she didn't look at him, she shivered in fear, her eyes locked on the floor. He then laughed in a child-like fashion and said, "It's okay, Mom, don't look at me, just keep listening. I cry for you all the time, you know. I cry when they cut me, when they clip my fingers off one by one. I cry for you when they sink their razor-sharp teeth into my skin, and I cry for you when they whisper hard truths in my ears. Although... I don't always have ears to hear..."

Evelyn slowly looked up and made eye contact. She was truly broken, but she got a few tear-clogged words out. "I am so sorry," she whispered.

"Sorry? You're sorry? Wow, when the hell did this happen? When are you ever sorry?" David hissed sarcastically. He stood up and towered over Evelyn as she remained a crying mess on the kitchen floor. "This is different. It was always you towering over me. You should be where I am." He was calm, relaxed, ghoulish once again, the sinister smile returned to his face. "I was actually not that surprised to find Dad down there. He tells me you'll be joining us real soon."

He began to laugh as he loomed over her, and she was too terrified to pick herself up off the ground. When she finally summoned the bravery to look up he was gone.

Evelyn got up and quickly walked into her bedroom. She closed the door and locked it behind her, then dropped to her knees. It finally all came out, every possible tear that could be cried. She wept like she had never wept before and held her head tightly with both hands. She whispered sorry to her Lord and Savior over and over again as she pulled tiny chunks of her hair out.

It was her deepest secret, the worst sin she had ever committed, that she brought death to her child. But she never truly thought that she was killing David or her husband. They were Demons, using illusion and intimidation to keep her from Jesus. She would have never killed any human being, only evil.

The rest of the day for the Singleton children was a good day. Ruth and Faith were happy as could be playing with Tiny. They were convinced that no cat on the face of the planet had ever felt as loved as Tiny. James was off and on between playing his video games and going for walks around the neighborhood. It was his way to relax and allow his imagination to take over.

The hours passed by and it grew dark outside. Faith and Ruth fell fast asleep together, Tiny roamed the Singleton household, and James was in a deep sleep.

The clock struck 3:27 a.m. when James suddenly woke up in the middle of the night.

As his eyes opened up, he looked around his room. It was nearly pitch black and not a single sound could be heard in the house except for the cat roaming around the house. Everybody else was fast asleep.

James turned over, closed his eyes, and attempted to fall asleep again. But the sounds of the cat playing in the living room were distracting to him.

He was starting to get that itch.

More than anything, he wanted to fall asleep, but his mind was running a million miles a minute. He wanted to hurt Tiny, he didn't understand why. Nobody would ever know, they were all fast asleep.

As he laid down with his eyes closed, he fought really hard to dismiss his dark thoughts. But he couldn't do it. His desire to harm the cat grew with every sound it made. He saw visions of opening it's tiny stomach and pulling strings of guts out of the carcass. He could see the blood coating his fingers. He envisioned himself cleaning a bloody pocket knife in the bathroom sink, watching blood swirling in a circle down the drain.

These thoughts were getting far too loud.

But they weren't nearly as loud as the clawing and bumping against his bedroom door. Tiny was once again meowing and trying to make her way into his bedroom. She couldn't have chosen a worse time to crave love and attention.

He kept his eyes closed and tried his best to ignore the quiet scratching that demanded his attention.

But Tiny kept scratching, and James kept thinking. She kept meowing, and he kept thinking. It was driving him crazy!

He sat up quickly and realized his heart was beating very rapidly. His clock read 3:48 a.m. Climbing out of his bed, he opened the door and allowed Tiny to happily walk into his room.

He picked her up gently and placed her on top of his bed. He pulled his flashlight from under his bed and shined it on the cat. He just stared at her for a while. She looked innocent, vulnerable, and so peaceful. She was curled up in a tiny ball, cuddled right next to him and happily purring, falling into a peaceful sleep.

As he kept the light on her, the temptation he felt was screaming louder than anything he had ever heard before. He hated this feeling, not the feeling of letting loose, but the feeling of fighting what was inside of him clawing to get out.

Tiny was fast asleep, and James watched over her like a hawk watched its prey. He knew if he wanted to do anything, nobody would hear it over the sound of his fan.

Finally, he grew tired of the screaming in his head. He moved the blanket off of him to the side, raising the flashlight high over his head. With full force, he pounded the top of Tiny's little head with the flashlight.

As he continued to beat her head over and over with the blunt object in his hand, he could see his white bedsheet turn red. He could hear the skull crack with every strike he made. The feeling was absolutely exhilarating to him.

He laid Tiny's tiny body out on the middle of his bedsheets. He was disturbed, but he couldn't help but feel released. He knew he wouldn't need to do this again for a while. This moment was enough to cleanse his mind for a few months. He would still have his secret thoughts and cravings, but it would take some time before they started to scream louder than the thoughts he wanted to have.

Quietly, he got out of his bed and took a long look at the mess he created. He was afraid of the new feeling burgeoning that he wanted to cut her open, but he also didn't want to take things further so quickly. He stood there frozen, disturbed, and knew that he needed to sneak her outside quietly.

As James quietly wrapped Tiny's body up in his white bedsheet, he thought about how lucky he was not to have stained his mattress. He held the kitten's limp body close to him as he quietly opened his bedroom door. The idea of someone seeing him was terrifying, but the sensation of having a secret was strangely exciting. He snuck down the hallway, made it to the front door, and opened it. As he stepped outside into the peaceful night, he was surprised by how wonderful the weather felt.

He walked to the sidewalk, admiring the beauty of the sky. The night sky was wonderfully lit up by its countess stars. The moon watched over him, following him as he walked the path down the silent street.

He knew where he was going. In fact, he had known where he was going to end up the second Tiny was brought into the house. It was just that he didn't want to have to go there again.

His destination was just a straight walk up the sidewalk, cutting through a house's backyard, and then through the dark woods behind house 301 Blacksmith Arch.

He entered the woods with his bloody flashlight leading the way, though he knew where he was going even without the light's assistance. He traveled deeper and deeper into the woods until he found a wooden plank in the ground. He placed Tiny's sheet wrapped carcass on the ground and began to dig into the dirt with the plank. He positioned his flashlight on a pile of leaves so that he wouldn't have to balance it awkwardly as he dug.

Eventually, dirty fur surfaced from the hole he was digging, and he knew that he was close. He continued to dig for a few more minutes until his hole was complete. When he stood up and shone his light into the hole he once again felt disturbed by what he'd done.

There were three carcasses already in the hole. They were nearly decomposed, but it was still obvious that they had been cut up and suffered from stab wounds.

James kept Tiny wrapped in his bedsheet and placed her into the hole. He took one last look at the disturbing scene before he filled the space back up with dirt. It only took him a few minutes to cover the dead cat, possum, and squirrel with dirt. Afterward, as a final touch, he placed the wooden plank into the ground as a decoy.

He played back his moments with those other two other corpses in his head as he walked back home in the night. The squirrel and possum were roadkill, but he had been fascinated by their dead bodies lying in the road. He felt like a freak for picking up the decomposed roadkill, but he had. He took them into the woods, carved into them, poked holes into them, but they had already been dead for quite some time. He still felt like he didn't truly know what they looked like inside because they weren't fresh. Tiny was the only animal he actually killed, so this was a different feeling.

He couldn't cry, and he felt bad about this. He felt a strange mixture of emotions and not all of it was guilt. Some of it was a rush, while some of it was truly disturbing. He hoped to God that nobody was awake when he made it home. When he found himself outside of the Singleton home, it looked pretty intimidating by the way the moon reflected off of it. He took a deep breath and quietly stepped inside.

The house was still quiet except for the gentle sound of everyone's fans, and he walked down the hallway into the bathroom. It was similar to the vision that he kept in his mind as he washed his hands in the bathroom sink. Blood and dirt were carried by water in a circular motion down the drain. He cleaned off the flashlight, as well, and made sure to leave no trace of anything in the sink before returning to his bedroom.

He couldn't believe that nobody had woken up, but he knew that he was lucky. He didn't have to explain himself to anyone. Going to his dresser, he grabbed another white bedsheet and spread it over his mattress. The clock read 5 a.m. and he knew that nobody would be awake for another few hours. He climbed back into bed, dismissed any thoughts of what happened, and fell into a peaceful sleep...

James woke up the next morning to the cries of Ruth. She was freaking out about Tiny somehow escaping overnight. Evelyn was comforting her, and Faith stood by completely dumbfounded. The fact that he felt a complete lack of compassion towards this disturbed him. As Ruth cried and the others comforted her, the doorbell rang.

Evelyn calmed Ruth down long enough to answer the door. A handsome man with long black hair stood across from her. He looked like he could be in his mid 30's. A black leather jacket, with a white T-shirt underneath, black relaxed fit jeans, and boots was what he wore. This man also had a silver cross necklace that stood out at first glance.

He smiled at her and charmingly said, "Good morning Evelyn, my name is Samuel."

Chapter 13
Samuel

"You trust me don't you?" asked Samuel as he gently placed his hand on the side of Jennifer's face. The tips of his fingers were sweetly tangling up in her red hair.

She tearfully looked into his blue eyes and said, "Of course I do."

Samuel moved his long black hair to the side because it covered one of his eyes. He stared intently into her soul and whispered, "Then show me."

But Jennifer showed hesitation. They both stood together in the large basement of someone's gigantic suburban home. A dim light hung from the middle of the ceiling and lit perfectly on its target. Three little girls were tied up and gagged in the middle of the basement. All three resembled their mother with red hair, and none of them looked a day over ten.

Samuel hovered behind Jennifer with his arms romantically wrapped around her. He softly kissed her cheek and soothingly rubbed her arms. Even though he was shirtless and appeared to be lean, he came across as dangerous because of the pistol tucked into the waist of his black skinny jeans. He used physical touch as a means to mellow her out and create an atmosphere of calm in the midst of chaos.

Jennifer's three daughters were quiet, even submissive to their plight. They had tears slowly rolling down their cheeks but maintained a sense of composure.

"I want you to demonstrate the love you have for me. I need you to show me that you will do anything for me," said Samuel as he continued to gently kiss her cheek. He then charismatically drifted toward her three daughters and ungagged them. As he calmly kneeled before them, making eye contact with them one at a time, he smiled. They all smiled back and expressed their love and trust towards him.

"I'm ok with this. I trust you, Samuel," said the girl in the middle. The other two nodded in agreement and both of them told him they loved him, too.

"I love all three of you from the bottom of my heart," said Samuel as he kissed the three on the top of their heads. He charmingly made his way back to Jennifer and handed her a pistol. With a soft kiss to her lips, he said, "I only need one of them, Jen."

Jennifer's once silent cries were now growing louder and more distinct. She held her face with both hands and cried, "I know, but it's so hard."

"I know it is, but it's going to be okay," he said softly. Samuel remained calm and slowly made his way back to the three daughters. He looked at the one in the middle and asked, "Haven't I always taken care of you, Heather?"

Heather, the oldest of the girls, nodded her head and smiled at him.

"You told me that night that you wanted a new father. I kissed the bruises on your arm," said Samuel as he gently kissed her arm where one of the bruises had been.

Heather broke down into tears and said, "He wouldn't stop touching me, and you made it stop."

Samuel embraced her and whispered, "Just like I promised I would. So you know I wouldn't lie. Look at me, from daughter to father... Do you see lying in my eyes?"

"No," replied Heather.

Samuel smiled and stepped away. There appeared to be a group of others circling them in the basement. There were four others, and Jennifer made five. Samuel looked at all of those in attendance and proceeded to speak loud and confident. "You all know this is the only way. A family needs to have complete trust in each other. I would lay my life down for each and every one of you. I have saved you all from this wicked world. It has to be us. God doesn't help anyone. He doesn't care at all. This is so much bigger than us, it is never goodbye."

The room then remained silent with no objections.

He walked toward Jennifer and told her it was time.

She raised the gun up with trembling hands and pointed it at her children. The moment grew tense and her children started to weep. There was still hesitation in Jennifer. Her hand shook uncontrollably. She couldn't bring herself to choose one for Samuel.

"God asked this of Abraham, Jen! It was cruel and pointless to do it for him. But for me... No... Us! This is about devotion, all of your children are ready to play their part. It's ok," said Samuel.

But Jennifer cried harder, and even in their fear, her kids screamed it was ok.

"I need to know that I am everything to you, Jen. I only need one!" yelled Samuel.

Jennifer wept, said she was sorry, and shot herself in the head. The moment the shot was fired all three of her children started to scream. In the following blur of noise and commotion, it wasn't real to Samuel yet. All of the others in the room were in pure shock and didn't know what to do next.

Samuel calmly walked over to Jennifer's corpse and picked up the gun that rested in a pool of blood. He looked at Jennifer's three children and said, "I need you guys to calm down. I need you to be strong for me."

But all three of them continued to weep. He took a deep breath with his head down and said, "Girls, I really need you to pull yourself together and show me that you are strong." Still, the screaming and weeping continued.

Samuel looked toward the back at one of the others present in the basement. It was a man by the name of Mason. He was in his mid 20's and had dirty long hair. It didn't reach his shoulders, but it was long enough to cover his eyes. Fit but not muscular, Mason appeared lean. He wore a thin long sleeve shirt with red and black horizontal stripes. His blue jeans looked worn with holes where the knees once were. He had the appearance of an early 90's grunge rock star.

"Mason, you know this isn't going to work. They can't calm down, they aren't strong enough to be with us," said Samuel.

Mason, disappointed, said, "I know Samuel, this isn't good for us."

The screaming was louder than ever, and the moment had grown chaotic and disturbing. Samuel sighed to himself, got up, and started to move to the stairs. When he brushed past Mason he murmured, "Handle this."

Mason softly nodded his head and Samuel made his way upstairs.

One day later... a few days after David Singleton's funeral...

Samuel was at the head of the long table in his giant kitchen. The wood was smooth and shiny, obviously expensive. A beautiful crystal chandelier hung above it, and expensive art portraits hung on the walls. The other four people who were in the basement were also sitting at the table: Mason, Luna, Connor, and Ava.

Luna, a woman in her early 20's, was skinny with black hair. She had a hipster look to her where she dressed colorful and expressive. Ava, in her late 20's, had short brown hair, and her look fit her perfectly. She wore black jeans and a tank top for a popular metal band. She had tattoos that covered both of her arms. Her look resembled Mason's look. Connor was the youngest one. He was a tatted up 19-year-old punk rocker. He was tall and skinny, and he wore beanies that covered his long black hair. His ears were pierced, and he sat silently at the table, fidgeting with a knife.

"We'll... I believe we are down by four," said Samuel, breaking the silence at the table. "Luckily, I maintained contact with two teenagers online. They are very interested in what we are and where we are going. I gave them a little something to do. Initiation..."

He looked around at all the others and saw that nobody was speaking. "If anybody has anything to say, please speak up. We are family and we need to be building on a foundation of honesty," Samuel reminded.

Luna broke the silence to tell Samuel that the kids were too young to be killed.

"I agree with you, Luna, they were too young to die. It absolutely broke my heart to watch it play out that way," said Samuel.

Luna remained calm and collected, and it was hard to tell that she was against Samuel's decision. She spoke up again and said, "Well, Samuel, if you felt that way, it doesn't make any sense at all to do what you did."

"I did it," said Mason.

Samuel held his hand up, signaling for Mason to stand down. He looked at Luna and began to mellowly explain himself.

"What we do is important. What we represent is important. We are the outcasts, saving the other outcasts. There is a church on every corner trying to 'save the lost,' but they are the ones lost. Every family in America is made of worthless puppets. But, every once in a while, you find someone special.

They are actually different. Unique to say the least. That's how we got here today. We came together. A common idea, a common purpose, we are in complete sync."

"What does that have to do with us killing children, Samuel?" demanded Luna as she grew frustrated.

Samuel was mellow and unphased by the tough question. He was confident in what he represented, and he knew he could win her over. "It's not about killing children, Luna, it's about staying focused on the mission. It's about nobody being divided, but being together as one functioning body. We need to all be on the same page and believe in one vision."

Luna was growing silent and submissive, yet still appeared unsure. Samuel sensed this and continued to speak. "A house divided is a house that falls. Those girls would have never been able to do what we do. They had a weak mother who probably had a lot to do with their weakness. We are trying to build something. We can't afford to question loyalty."

"Remind me again what we are building Samuel," replied Luna.

He smiled at her indulgently and replied in his charming manner, "A family. Which brings me to why we are here today. We need more brothers, more sisters, more mothers, more fathers. I am about to leave you guys for a bit so that I can bring home your new family."

"That's wonderful, but who do you have in mind Samuel?" asked Connor as he continued to fidget with his knife.

"I was driving around town and saw a lineup of cars being led by police. I knew right away it was a funeral. I followed them because the only cure for a lack of family is the presence of family. I wanted to see if I felt anything for anyone. If I could find someone special who needed us in this time of grieving. As luck has it... I found a few people," replied Samuel.

"Who are they?" asked Ava.

Samuel took a deep breath and said, "The Singletons. It's a mother without her oldest son, two daughters without an older brother, and a socially awkward boy without his older brother's guidance. Nobody saw me, I was in the back. But, I was moved with compassion when I saw them. They appeared broken and I believe they need us. They just don't know it yet."

"I'm assuming you followed them and found out where they stay?" asked Mason, cracking his knuckles.

Samuel innocently chuckled and told him, "Of course."

The moment seemed less tense and everyone appeared to be compassionate toward the idea of a broken family in need. Samuel got out of his chair and began to slowly pace the room around the table. He was mellow, silent, trying to find his closing words. He stopped when he finally knew what to say.

"I sought every single one of you out because I love that deeply. You met me face to face and I shared my heart with you. I helped you discover purpose when you felt hopeless. If anyone was keeping you from being saviors of this God-forsaken world, I took care of it. I am going to simply drive to their house, greet them, and they will let me in. They will let me in because they need someone to listen. They are searching for something that will find its way to them. It's their lucky day."

"And it will be the most beautiful thing that has ever happened to them," said Ava.

Samuel smiled at her and said, "I am going to make them a part of something bigger than themselves. They will be one of us. I don't expect to be away long, but I'll be gone as long as it takes. When I come back, we will have more family to look after. Trust me on this."

"Can we have the names of our new brother and sisters?" asked Luna.

"Evelyn is the broken mother. She grieves the loss of her child. She is outspoken and strong from what I gathered at the funeral. She could make a good leader if we have patience. Ruth is the youngest daughter, and she appears to take after Evelyn. If I can connect with her mom, then I will have no problem with her. Faith is the oldest daughter. Sweet and quiet. I see pain in her eyes. Then there's James... I see a younger me in him."

"What about the two teenagers online? The task you have them doing?" inquired Mason.

Samuel smiled and maintained his confidence. He calmly replied, "I got word of a church lock-in. All college-aged. It's only them, no students, no congregation. The two I have been speaking with are going to join and determine who amongst them values life the most. Not only their life but life for what it really is. They have my number and you have mine, as well. Just be ready to pick up our new family when I call."

Mason said nothing else, he just simply nodded.

As Samuel closed out, he left the room and grabbed the keys to his car. He felt confident that he would achieve what he set out to do. He was going to build his family and walk in accordance with his purpose.

At the door, he stopped, turned around, and saw the others standing together. They were smiling and waving goodbye to their leader. "Take care of them for me Mason. I'll be back before you know it and then we can get things moving. As a family..."

End of book one.

CONTINUE THE STORY
WITH "AN ANTI-RELIGIOUS CULT SEQUEL"
AVAILABLE NOW AT AMAZON & KINDLEUNLIMITED

Dylan Colón

This House Is Broken Part 2

Evelyn is no longer the only danger to her children. There is now a charismatic cult leader at her front door. He is Samuel, the leader of "The Church Of Forsaken Angels".

They are responsible for religious hate crimes and multiple church shootings. Evelyn is an abusive mother who runs her household like a religious tyrant. Samuel is the leader of a murderous cult that oppresses the religious for religion's oppression of others. What's to happen next?

Also Available
*Amazon
*kindleunlimited

The story of MY LIFE
and I hope it HELPS!
DareToDream.

DYLAN COLÓN

TRAUMA TAKES A LOSS

MY STORY, MY TRAUMA, OUR HEALING

I'm not a therapist...
I'm just a regular guy, willing to share my story.

I hope my scars help heal your scars. Traumatic breakups, life without a parent, being bullied, struggling with a learning disability, toxic people, coping with death, depression, anxiety, suicidal thoughts and tendencies... and how I overcome it all!

HELP ME OUT?

IF YOU'D LIKE TO BE A PART OF MY JOURNEY AND DREAM AS AN AUTHOR... PLEASE LEAVE AN HONEST REVIEW ON AMAZON! THE MORE REVIEWS I HAVE, THE MORE LIKELY MY NOVEL IS SEEN ON THE AMAZON MARKET! I WELCOME ALL THOUGHTS ABOUT MY WORK. BOTH GOOD AND BAD!
-DYLAN

DARETODREAM

Made in the USA
Monee, IL
27 March 2022

b0c6275e-ac34-4ed2-86f6-8ea0c0ff1244R01